T

Paddy's Promise

A Tess and Tilly Mystery

by

Kathi Daley

This book is a work of fiction. Names, characters, places, and incidents either are products of the author's imagination or are used fictitiously. Any resemblance to actual events or locales or persons, living or dead, is entirely coincidental.

Copyright © 2019 by Katherine Daley

Version 1.0

All rights reserved, including the right of reproduction in whole or in part in any form.

Special Dedication

This book is dedicated to the group of tireless JDRF volunteers who raised money for type 1 diabetes research. A special thank-you to Jay Snyder, who bid on the chance to name a character in an upcoming Kathi Daley book. Jay chose the name Jennifer Anne, for his daughter.

To learn more about JDRF please visit their website: https://www.jdrf.org/

I want to thank the very talented Jessica Fischer for the cover art.

I so appreciate Bruce Curran, who is always ready and willing to answer my cyber questions; Jayme Maness for helping out with the book clubs; and Peggy Hyndman for helping sleuth out those pesky typos.

And, of course, thanks to the readers and bloggers in my life, who make doing what I do possible.

Thank you to Randy Ladenheim-Gil for the editing.

And finally, I want to thank my husband Ken for allowing me time to write by taking care of everything else.

Books by Kathi Daley

Come for the murder, stay for the romance.

Zoe Donovan Cozy Mystery:

Halloween Hijinks
The Trouble With Turkeys
Christmas Crazy
Cupid's Curse
Big Bunny Bump-off
Beach Blanket Barbie
Maui Madness
Derby Divas
Haunted Hamlet
Turkeys, Tuxes, and Tabbies
Christmas Cozy
Alaskan Alliance
Matrimony Meltdown
Soul Surrender
Heavenly Honeymoon
Hopscotch Homicide
Ghostly Graveyard
Santa Sleuth
Shamrock Shenanigans
Kitten Kaboodle
Costume Catastrophe
Candy Cane Caper
Holiday Hangover
Easter Escapade
Camp Carter
Trick or Treason
Reindeer Roundup

Hippity Hoppity Homicide
Firework Fiasco
Henderson House
Holiday Hostage
Lunacy Lake – *Coming in 2019*

Zimmerman Academy The New Normal
Zimmerman Academy New Beginnings
Ashton Falls Cozy Cookbook

Tj Jensen Paradise Lake Mysteries by Henery Press:

Pumpkins in Paradise
Snowmen in Paradise
Bikinis in Paradise
Christmas in Paradise
Puppies in Paradise
Halloween in Paradise
Treasure in Paradise
Fireworks in Paradise
Beaches in Paradise
Thanksgiving in Paradise – *Coming in 2019*

Whales and Tails Cozy Mystery:

Romeow and Juliet
The Mad Catter
Grimm's Furry Tail
Much Ado About Felines
Legend of Tabby Hollow
Cat of Christmas Past
A Tale of Two Tabbies
The Great Catsby
Count Catula

The Cat of Christmas Present
A Winter's Tail
The Taming of the Tabby
Frankencat
The Cat of Christmas Future
Farewell to Felines
A Whisker in Time
The Catsgiving Feast
A Whale of a Tail – *Coming in 2019*

Writers' Retreat Southern Seashore Mystery:

First Case
Second Look
Third Strike
Fourth Victim
Fifth Night
Sixth Cabin
Seventh Chapter
Eighth Witness

Rescue Alaska Paranormal Mystery:

Finding Justice
Finding Answers
Finding Courage
Finding Christmas
Finding Shelter – *Coming in 2019*

A Tess and Tilly Mystery:
The Christmas Letter
The Valentine Mystery
The Mother's Day Mishap
The Halloween House
The Thanksgiving Trip
The Saint Paddy's Promise

The Inn at Holiday Bay:
Boxes in the Basement
Letters in the Library
Message in the Mantel – *April 2019*

Family Ties:
The Hathaway Sisters
Harper
Harlow – *May 2019*

Haunting by the Sea:
Homecoming by the Sea
Secrets by the Sea
Missing by the Sea
Betrayal by the Sea – *March 2019*

Sand and Sea Hawaiian Mystery:
Murder at Dolphin Bay
Murder at Sunrise Beach
Murder at the Witching Hour
Murder at Christmas
Murder at Turtle Cove
Murder at Water's Edge
Murder at Midnight

Seacliff High Mystery:
The Secret
The Curse
The Relic
The Conspiracy
The Grudge
The Shadow
The Haunting

Road to Christmas Romance:
Road to Christmas Past

Chapter 1

Sunday, March 17

Five dogs in training, two human trainers, one canine trainer, a beautiful sunny sky, and a rarely seen high temperature of sixty-two degrees made for what I considered to be an almost perfect March day.

"Oliver Hanson, this is Tess Thomas and her dog Tilly," Dr. Brady Baker, the owner of the only veterinary hospital and animal shelter in my hometown of White Eagle, Montana, introduced the tall, dark-haired man who had approached from the far side of the parking lot. "Oliver is interested in adopting Hank and would like to watch our training session today."

"I'm happy to meet you." I held out my hand in greeting. "Hank is a great dog. He has the usual energy one might expect from a sixteen-month-old lab, but Brady and I have been working with him for almost two months now, and the improvement we've seen in his responses to verbal commands as well as his overall attention span has been amazing."

I couldn't help but notice the way the man's eyes twinkled when he smiled. "I'm glad to hear it. The main reason I came all the way from Spokane to adopt a rescue from the shelter in White Eagle is because of the work you do training your dogs before you place them. I have to say, I am more than just a little impressed."

I glanced at Brady and grinned. Brady and I put in a lot of hours training the dogs here, and we were both proud of our accomplishments. "Brady and I realize that a dog who has received at least basic training will be less likely to find his way back to the shelter once he has been adopted." I looked toward a bench in the sun. "You picked a good day to make the trip. Why don't you have a seat, and after we put all the dogs through their paces, you can try working with Hank one-on- one."

The man nodded. "That would be great. Thank you."

I'm not usually one to brag, but I will say that Brady, Tilly, and I have worked out a training routine that by this point runs like clockwork. In as little as eight to ten weeks, we can take an undisciplined and untrained dog and turn him or her into one who will listen to his or her human and respond correctly to the basic commands of come, sit, down, stay, heel, and wait. Most dogs are cleared for adoption after the basic training course, but there are those with unique potential that we hold back for specialty training that could make them a candidate for advanced work with FEMA or another organization that utilizes highly trained canines.

Brady and I had tried a few different approaches in the beginning, but then we found that the key to our success in many cases was Tilly. Tilly is an old pro when it comes to responding to both verbal commands and hand signals, and we have often used her to demonstrate the behavior we are after, which seems to help the younger dogs who are eager to learn but have no idea what it is we are asking of them.

The dogs we'd brought out with us today seemed to be enjoying the warm weather and sunshine as much as their human trainers. Almost everyone was on their best behavior, which made the training session seem to go faster. In another couple of months, we'd add water training at the lake for many of the more advanced dogs. It was surprising how many of our prospective parents wanted to adopt dogs who liked the water and could swim.

"It seems to me that Rosie is becoming more and more distracted with each session," I said to Brady as we loaded the dogs other than Hank into his truck after our session. "When we first started working with her, she showed real promise, but now I'm just not sure."

Brady huffed out a breath. "Yeah. I've noticed that as well. Maybe some one-on-one time will help get her back on track. I'll work with her this week. Why don't you take Hank and get Oliver started with his individual session while I finish up here?"

"Okay. Do you know if Oliver has experience training a young dog?"

"When I asked him that question, he said that his last dog lived for an impressive seventeen years and he was a child when he was trained, so Hank will be his first."

"Okay. I'll go over the basics."

I instructed Tilly to stay with Brady, then headed across the parking lot with Hank on a lead. Oliver stood up to greet us as we approached.

"Oliver, this is Hank."

Hank wagged his whole body as Oliver stooped down to pet him.

"Hank is still in what I refer to as the puppy stage despite his size," I informed the man. "He has a strong play instinct, which can seem to many to be a negative, but if you understand his need for exercise, you can use it to your advantage."

"Oh, and how is that?" he asked as he ruffled Hank behind the ears.

"A lot of dogs respond best to food as a reward for a job well done, but Hank will do almost anything for a chance to play with you for even a few minutes. The trick is to use playtime as a reward for cooperative behavior. Hank wants to please you. If you make it clear what you are asking of him and reward that behavior with a tug-of-war session or a game of fetch, I think you will both be very happy. I'm going to have you put him through his paces today. When the session is over, if he has done well, let him know you are happy with his behavior and then play with him for a few minutes."

Oliver nodded. "Okay, let's give it a try."

"We'll start easy with a down stay and then work on recall and finally walking at heel."

As I knew he would, Hank performed like a pro. When it came time for his play session, it looked as if Oliver was having as much fun as the dog. I think we'd found a match that had the potential to last a lifetime. Oliver agreed to return the following weekend for another session, and if that went well, he would take Hank home with him after the adoption paperwork was completed.

"Do you need a ride?" Brady asked after Oliver left to drive back to Washington and we'd completed our training for the day.

"No. Tony dropped me off and was going to pick me up, but I told him he could just pick me up later from Bree's. If Tilly and I cut through the park, it is less than a mile to her place, and it is such a beautiful day that I thought we'd walk."

Brady looked up toward the clear blue sky. "It is a nice day. How is the wedding planning coming along?"

I shrugged. "It's coming along exactly as I predicted it would."

"As you predicted?"

I looked Brady in the eye. "Stressful, angst-filled, drama at its best. On the day we found out that Mike and Bree were getting married, I told Tony that Bree would start off by swearing that she wasn't going to be one of those bridezillas she professes to have no patience for, while I predicted that halfway in, she'd be as monsterlike as any bride who had ever existed."

Brady laughed. "Is she really that bad?"

"She really is. But it is her wedding. And as her best friend, maid of honor, and future sister-in-law, I want her to have her perfect day. If she is having a hard time figuring out exactly what that day might look like, I am determined to be patient and let her take the time she needs."

"You're a good friend."

"Bree means a lot to me. She has always been like a sister to me, and now that she is going to be my real sister, I couldn't be happier." I tossed the stack of traffic cones we used in training into the back of Brady's truck. "Are we doing another training session on Saturday?"

"I'd planned on it. I thought we could just meet here if the weather is nice again. If we are back to regular March weather, we'll meet at the shelter. I want to get as many dogs through our basic training as possible before the adoption clinic next month."

"Are you still thinking of doing speed dating again?"

Brady nodded. "It seemed to work well the last time we tried it, so yeah, I thought we could give it another go."

"Okay, then, I'll see you on Saturday if not before." After waving to Brady, Tilly and I took off across the park. I loved this time of the year, when the snow had melted and everything felt fresh and new. It had been an early spring this year and I supposed we could very well get more snow, but I knew once the heating trend started, any snow that did fall would melt in a matter of hours. Mike and Bree had decided to get married in June. I knew my brother would prefer a church wedding and an indoor reception, but Bree wanted to be married outdoors under the night sky. Her plan seemed to me to be riddled with problems, but I knew she needed to work through those problems herself, so I just stood back and supported her process.

Of course, in my mind, the biggest challenge was the weather. June could be tricky. Sometimes the month was warm and mild, while other Junes could be wet and cool. In terms of snowpack, it had been a mild winter this year. We'd had snow early on, but then it seemed to taper off, with only small storms blowing in during the normally heavy snowfall months. I supposed that a warmish winter and spring could mean that summer would arrive early. June could be gorgeous in White Eagle if the planets aligned and everything fell into place.

I glanced toward the walking path that meandered through the park. The trees were budding, and I knew that the brown and barren landscape would begin to turn green with just a few more warm days. The flowering shrubs were beginning to bud, and if the temperature cooperated, the entire park would be brilliant, with flowers in a multitude of colors before long. I glanced down at Tilly, who began to wag her tail so hard that it was swatting my leg. Pausing to see what she was looking at, I noticed a young woman with long blond hair sitting on a bench next to an elderly woman holding a cane. The young woman smiled at Tilly and me as we approached.

"Can I pet your dog?" the young woman asked.

"Certainly. Tilly loves to meet new people." I motioned to Tilly that she could carefully approach the woman, who had reached out a hand.

"I just love dogs, and yours is beautiful." The woman smiled. "My name is Jennifer Anne Claremont, and this is my grandmother, Elizabeth Bradford."

"I'm Tess Thomas and this is Tilly. We are both happy to meet you." I glanced toward the lake, which had been frozen until the warm weather we'd been having had arrived. "It's a beautiful day to get outdoors."

"It really is. And I am so grateful for the sunshine and warm temperature. I can't tell you how many

Saint Patrick's days Nana and I have spent sitting on this bench in the middle of a snowstorm."

"You sit out here every year despite the weather?" I asked.

Jennifer Anne turned her head to the side and glanced at her grandmother with a look of complete adoration on her face. "Have to. Nana has made the pilgrimage to this bench every March 17 for the past sixty years, rain, snow, or sunshine. I started coming with her eight years ago, after she suffered a stroke that limited her mobility and made it impossible for her to drive. It is also difficult for her to speak, which makes any sort of public transportation difficult, so I volunteered to chauffer her for as long as she needs me."

From the woman's loving expression, I didn't think she minded the duty she had volunteered for in the least. It warmed my heart to see such a devoted granddaughter. I no longer had a grandmother, and in the moment, it really hit home how much I'd been missing out on.

"Sixty years?" I responded. "That's quite a run. I sense there's a story behind it."

Jennifer Anne glanced at her grandmother. "Is it okay if I tell Tess and Tilly your story?"

The white-haired woman nodded.

Jennifer Anne turned back to where I was standing. "It's kind of a long story, so you might want to take a seat."

I sat down on a nearby bench, and Tilly sat at my feet.

The granddaughter settled back as well. "Sixty years ago today, my grandmother was supposed to meet the one true love of her life at this very bench so they could run away and start a new life together, but he never showed up."

My smile faded. "Oh no. What happened?"

The light in Jennifer Anne's eyes faded just a bit. "Nana doesn't know." She glanced at the woman sitting next to her. "What she does know is that Patrick O'Malley, the man for whom Nana had professed her love and agreed to marry, originally came to this area the previous summer with friends who'd rented a cabin and planned to spend their time hiking and fishing. By the time the summer came to an end, Patrick was madly in love with my grandmother, and when his friends left, he stayed. They grew even closer as winter set in, and by Valentine's Day, they knew they wanted to spend the rest of their lives together, even though my grandmother's family didn't approve of her relationship with Patrick and he assured her that his wouldn't be any happier. They decided to defy their families and became engaged."

I couldn't help but notice Elizabeth's hand tighten on her cane. She may not be able to speak, but I could see that she still felt strongly about the events that had taken place all those years ago.

Jennifer Anne continued. "Shortly after he professed his intention to spend his life with her, Patrick told my grandmother that he needed to return home for a short time to take care of some business and to notify his family of his intention to wed and to move permanently out west. Nana still lived at home, and she knew it would only cause problems with her very strict parents if Patrick came to the house looking for her, so the two agreed to meet here on this bench at two o'clock on Saint Patrick's Day. From here, they planned to simply disappear and live out their lives together."

"But he never showed up?"

Jennifer Anne's expression softened. She glanced at her grandmother with compassion. "No. He never showed up."

"And he never tried to contact your grandmother in any other way?" I asked.

"He didn't. Initially, Nana came to the park and waited on the bench every day, but eventually, she was forced to accept that he wasn't coming back for her, so she dealt with the fallout from their brief yet intense love affair and made do with what she had."

"Fallout?"

"Patrick left my grandmother with child. My mother was born just before Thanksgiving that same year. When Nana's parents found out she was pregnant, they kicked her out, and she was forced to find a way to provide for herself and her baby on her own. And she did. She moved to Polson, got a job waiting tables, gave birth to my mother, who she named Patricia, and made a life. For the most part, I think she pushed thoughts of Patrick into the back of her mind, but every year on March 17, no matter what else was going on her in life, she made the trip north to sit on this bench."

I placed my hand over my heart. How incredibly sad. "And your mother—does she ever come with you?"

Jennifer Anne shook her head. "My mother died years ago. She had me later in life and died from complications from an illness when I was only two. Grandma gave up her plans for retirement to raise me and to ensure that I'd have a good life. She had her stroke eight years ago, when I was just sixteen. When it came time for me to leave home and go to college, I decided to stay to take care of the woman who had sacrificed so much to raise me when I needed her." Jennifer Anne laced her fingers through the fingers of her grandmother's left hand and gave it a squeeze. "We make a good pair, the two of us. Don't we, Nana?"

It seemed to me that Elizabeth had a hard time smiling, but the love for her granddaughter that sparkled in her eyes was obvious.

"That is quite a story. It is both sad and beautiful. I have to wonder whether you have ever tried looking for Patrick."

Jennifer shook her head. "Sixty years ago, it wasn't so simple to look for someone who lived clear across the country unless you hired a private investigator. That took money that Nana didn't have. The thought has occurred to me to try now. I realize that after all this time Patrick may be dead, but I still think that it would give Nana comfort to have the answers she'd never been able to find on her own. But I'm not exactly a computer wiz, and I certainly don't have PI skills. I'd have no idea where to even start."

I smiled. "It just so happens that my boyfriend, Tony Marconi, *is* a computer wiz. With your permission, of course, I would be happy to ask him to try to find Patrick."

Jennifer Anne turned to her grandmother. "What do you think? Should we take a stab at it?"

Elizabeth paused, as if considering the offer. I watched as her gaze narrowed and her lips tightened. Eventually, she nodded her head slowly.

Jennifer Anne looked back to me. "Where would he start?"

"I guess he'd start with whatever you know."

Jennifer Anne frowned. "We don't know a lot. I've already told you his name, Patrick O'Malley. He told Grandma he was twenty-four when they met in 1959, so if he's still alive, he'd be around eighty-four now. His grandparents immigrated to the United States from Ireland at around the turn of the twentieth century, but she doesn't know exactly when. He never mentioned the first names of his parents or anyone else in his family to her. Nana said he referred to Boston as home, and that his parents owned their own business, though she didn't know what kind. One of the friends he came to White Eagle with that summer was about his age and his name was Toby Willis. She didn't know much about Toby other than that he'd been friends with Patrick for a long time."

"Did Patrick know he was going to be a father at the time he left town?" I figured I had to ask. It had occurred to me that he may simply have decided that fatherhood was not for him and had used the excuse to go home to slip away, skipping out on his responsibility.

"No. Nana didn't realize that she was pregnant until after they were to meet. They didn't have early pregnancy tests back then."

I realized that much was true. I took out my phone. "If you don't mind sharing your cell number, I'll text you mine. When I speak to Tony, he may have other questions for you. Do the two of you live here in White Eagle?"

"We both live in Polson."

"Okay. That's close enough." I looked directly at Elizabeth Bradford. "I can't guarantee we'll be able to find your answers, but I promise you that we will try."

Again, she didn't smile, but I could see there was moisture in her eyes.

Chapter 2

When Tilly and I arrived at Bree's home, I found her on the phone, and while I wasn't sure who she was speaking to, I could tell she wasn't at all happy. Not only was she pacing around the room but her naturally pale complexion was as red and ruddy as if she had spent the day in the sun.

"I sense a problem." I filled a dish with water for Tilly, then sat down at Bree's dining table after she'd hung up and turned to greet me.

"That was the caterer I'd hoped to hire. They said they are overbooked for the weekend I requested and are sorry to inform me that they will be unable to provide the food for my wedding. I have a feeling that they weren't actually overbooked and were just using that as an excuse. When I initially spoke to them, it seemed obvious they weren't really keen on catering a wedding that is going to take place so late in the evening."

"I know you have your heart set on a wedding under the stars, and I know you have selected June 21 as your date because it is the summer solstice, but it doesn't get dark until close to ten o'clock. That is really late for a wedding. And to try to have a meal after that is…" I wanted to say crazy but settled for "challenging."

Bree let out a long sigh. "I guess you're right. Exchanging our vows under the stars just sounded so romantic, and I chose the twenty-first because it felt sort of significant, being the solstice and all." Bree groaned. "I'm making this too complicated, aren't I?"

I put my hand over Bree's. "It's your wedding and I want you to have exactly what you have always dreamed of, and if having a reception at midnight is what needs to happen, you know I'll be there. Having said that, yeah, I do think you are making it too complicated. You will never find a caterer who is willing to serve that late in the evening, at least not in White Eagle, and I have a feeling that there could be a lot of guests who come up with conflicting plans as well. If getting married under the stars on the twenty-first of June is the most important thing to you, I think you should go for it, but you should probably keep it small. Maybe family only. We could have the wedding at Tony's place. A ceremony next to the lake would be magical. And after you exchange vows, Tony could prepare dinner for everyone. If," I continued, "on the other hand, it is more important for you to have a big wedding with all your friends and acquaintances present, I think you should plan an indoor affair during the day, or perhaps earlier in the evening. Or at least an outdoor affair with an indoor alternative like The Lakehouse, which has a beautiful beach if the weather is nice but also has a conference and event room if the weather turns out to be less than ideal."

Bree plopped down in the chair across from me. "Yeah. I'm hearing what you are saying. I guess The Lakehouse would be nice, if it is available. We could have the ceremony on the beach, weather permitting, and then we could have the reception on the patio. We could string lights, and by the time we got around to the dancing, it would be dark. I suppose that if Mike and I can't exchange our vows under the stars, we could at least have our first dance there."

"Or you could flip things around and have dinner first, say at eight o'clock, and then exchange vows after it grows dark, which, as I've said, I imagine should be around ten."

Bree's expression appeared uncertain. "You think? It would be sort of unconventional to exchange our vows after the meal."

I shrugged. "It is your wedding. Do what you want to do. Well, at least what you and Mike want to do."

My comment made Bree groan.

"I'm sensing yet another problem."

"It's not really a problem, it's just that every time I ask Mike about the wedding, he responds with the boilerplate response: he wants what I want. At first, I found his desire to make me happy sort of sweet. Now I just find it annoying. It's like he doesn't even care about our wedding."

I paused and then continued carefully. "He cares. I know Mike loves you and the day you exchange your vows is as important to him as it is to you, but guys don't always care about things like the type of flowers in the bouquet or the color of the bridesmaids' dresses, the way women often do. I think the most important thing to him, on the most important day of his life, is to have the certainty in his heart that he was able to gift the woman he cherishes with the wedding she'd always dreamed of."

Bree wiped a tear from her cheek. "I know you're right. I have let this wedding get to me in a way I'd vowed not to. I actually do realize that I am making not only myself but everyone around me crazy. Even my mother is losing patience, and she was so excited to be part of the planning when we started this journey. I'll call The Lakehouse, and if it is available on June 21, I'll arrange to go by with Mike for a look. Having the reception dinner before the exchange of vows isn't the craziest idea I've entertained. We can have our guests arrive at seven thirty for drinks, have dinner at eight, the ceremony at ten, and then dancing after."

I smiled. "I think that sounds like a perfectly lovely idea." Of course, I realized that for Bree to be married under the stars as she dreamed, the weather still needed to cooperate, but in my mind, it was best to tackle one obstacle at a time. "Any idea what time Mike is going to be by?"

"He had to go out on a call or he would have been here by now."

"I thought he was off today."

"He was," Bree confirmed, "but Frank called him in. He didn't go into details when he called to let me know he was going to be late, but from what he did say, I suspect there's been a murder."

"Murder?" I screeched. It seemed to me that Bree might have opened our conversation with this piece of news. "Did he say who the victim was?"

Bree shook her head. "No. All he really told me was that there had been a death in the community that Frank wanted his help dealing with. He never actually said it was a murder, but if it was a natural death, why would Frank call Mike in on his day off?"

That, I decided, was a good question. "I'm going to call Tony to see if he knows what's going on. If you want to grab your bridal magazines, we can look at place settings when I'm done."

"I'll get the magazines after I call The Lakehouse. If it isn't available, we'll need to focus our efforts on an alternate venue."

Bree headed into the kitchen, where she'd left her phone, and I called Tony. I didn't know for certain if he'd have heard what was going on, but I knew he was in town, so chances were he had heard and could fill me in.

"I take it you heard," Tony said when he answered his cell.

"Not really," I answered. "Bree just mentioned that Mike had to go out on a call and that someone had died. She didn't know who or how. I was hoping that you did."

"It's Brick Brannigan."

"Oh no." Brick owned the local bar. He was a nice and popular guy, despite his rough side. "What happened?"

"I don't have all the details, but from what I've been able to gather from comments I've overheard, it sounds as if he was shot in the chest, most likely as he cleaned up after closing last night."

I supposed it made sense that he'd been shot after closing and not earlier in the evening. If he'd been killed while he was still open, there would have been witnesses to the event. "Any idea who shot him or why?"

"None. Mike is inside, as is Frank. The new rookie they are training to help out when one of them is off came outside to meet the coroner when he arrived, and everything I've managed to pick up has been by listening in on their conversation. I suppose that once Mike is done there he'll be able to fill us in on the details."

"The rookie's name is Gage. He's just a kid and about as green as they come, but he tries. Have the crime scene guys from the county arrived yet?"

"No, not yet, but I'm sure they'll be along soon. When I first arrived, the parking area was deserted, but a crowd has begun to gather and it seems that everyone has an opinion as to what happened and why. Of course, it will be up to Mike and Frank to sort it all out. Do you want me to stay here and try to find out what is going on, or should I meet you at Bree's?"

"Bree is in one of her moods, so you might want to wait a bit before coming by. I'll text you and let you know when I've managed to turn things around and create a drama-free zone."

Tony laughed. "You are doing an excellent job as best friend and maid of honor. I'm not sure I would have been able to maintain the level of patience you have."

I smiled. "To be honest, I'm kind of surprised that I haven't had a meltdown of my own by now, but I actually think we are making progress today. I may even have talked her into starting the wedding earlier in the evening. I need to go before Bree changes her mind yet again. Text me if you hear anything, and I'll text you when it is safe to come over."

I spoke to Tony for another minute, then hung up just as Bree danced into the room.

"The Lakehouse has an opening on June 21 and they are willing to hold it for me for forty-eight hours so I can discuss it with Mike. I need to call him."

"I wouldn't. The murder he responded to was Brick Brannigan."

Bree's smile faded. "Brick? What happened?"

"Tony didn't have all the details, but from what he overheard, Brick was shot in the chest while he was cleaning up last night."

"Oh my God. Poor Brick. Who would do such a thing?"

I shrugged. "I suppose he could have gotten in an argument with someone. People do carry guns, and people who have been drinking don't always make the best decisions. Maybe there was even a witness. We'll need to wait until Mike gets here to find out what he knows."

Bree plopped down on the sofa. "Yeah. Mike will figure this out. He'll make sure that whoever killed Brick is made to pay."

"You might want to hold off on a discussion of the wedding plans until after Mike has a chance to decompress. Brick and Mike were friends. I think he is probably taking this hard."

"Of course. I'll wait and bring up the venue tomorrow." Bree folded her legs up under her body. "I guess we should have Tony come over now, rather than later. I doubt we'll get much wedding planning done and he should be here when Mike gets here. Is he in town?"

I nodded. "I'll call him back in a bit. He's hanging out at in the parking lot of the bar, trying to find out exactly what is going on. Maybe he can even get a word to Mike that we are all here for him when he is ready to leave."

******

By the time Mike arrived it was late, and I could see that he was both exhausted and torn up emotionally. I wanted to help, but I wasn't sure how to do that. Mike was good at his job and I knew he would find Brick's killer. But I also knew that having to maintain the professional distance that was required during a murder investigation was going to be difficult given the circumstances.

"Do you have any suspects?" I asked after Bree made Mike something to eat and we'd all gathered around the dining table.

"Not really. Frank and I interviewed those town residents we knew had been in the bar on Saturday evening. Everyone we spoke to seemed to think that Brick was in a good mood and hadn't had anything heavy on his mind, but we were close enough for me to know that even if something had been wrong, he wouldn't have brought his somber mood to work with him."

"And no one noticed anyone come in who seemed to have a grievance with him?"

Mike took a bite of his sandwich and washed it down with a swig of his cola. "No one has been willing to say as much. Of course, it was a busy

Saturday night and there had to have been dozens of customers in and out of the place. We've only been able to interview a handful of people so far, and those were mainly spectators who gathered in the parking lot to see what was going on when they noticed the emergency vehicles on the property. Frank is searching Brick's home as we speak, and I plan to head back over tonight as well. I figure I'll start by making a complete list of everyone who was in the bar from open to close. Someone had to have seen something."

"If you need any help, you know you just need to ask," I said.

"I know, but this is an open police investigation. I think it best if Frank and I handle things at this point."

After Mike ate, he headed over to the station to meet up with Frank, Bree claimed to have a headache and said she was heading to bed, and Tony and I said our goodbyes and headed to my cabin. I still had Tilly with me, but Tony's dog, Titan, was at the cabin, and we decided to take both dogs out for a quick run before we settled in for a night of gaming. Despite the warmth of the day, it had turned cold once the sun set, so we bundled up and grabbed our flashlights before setting out.

"What a roller coaster of a day," I said to Tony after we reached the frequently traveled trail near my cabin. "For me, it started out on such a high with our successful training session, followed by a fascinating conversation with new people I met in the park. I hit a bit of a bump when I first arrived at Bree's and found her on the phone yelling at the caterer, but we even managed to get her and her wedding plans back on track, so I felt like things were climbing once again.

And then to find out that Brick has been murdered… Talk about an unexpected plunge. I still can't believe it."

"Brick was a great guy, but the profession he chose wasn't exactly the safest one in the world."

"What do you mean?"

"Owning a bar and tending it yourself pretty much guarantees that you are going to spend a good amount of time in the presence of men and women who have been drinking. Many of Brick's customers will have come to the bar to celebrate a victory or milestone, but just as many most likely patronized the establishment to numb their emotions and drown their sorrows. It is not at all unusual for someone who has had too much to drink to turn violent, especially if they have been provoked in some way, or just think they have."

I leaned my head on Tony's shoulder. "Yeah. I guess you're right. I suppose that Brick's death could very well have been the result of a random event caused by a customer who drank a bit too much and went a little crazy. Still, it might also be that Brick died at the hands of someone who had not simply lost control of his emotions but had come to the bar with the intention of killing him."

"I guess that may be true as well. I imagine that Mike will sort it all out."

"I could tell he wanted us to stay out of it and let him handle things."

"That can be expected," Tony answered.

"Yeah." I sighed. "But Brick was a friend. It will be hard to stand back and not get my hands dirty."

"Has it occurred to you that by getting involved in Mike's active investigations, you are demonstrating that you don't have faith in his ability to do his job without you?"

I frowned. "Actually, I never looked at it that way. I guess I can understand how it might. Especially to Mike."

"I think it is best if we both take a step back and let him do his job. If he wants our help, he will ask for it."

I nodded and glanced up at Tony's face. "Okay. I will agree to take a step back, but perhaps we should change the subject."

Tony did just that. "So, you mentioned people that you met in the park."

"An elderly woman and her granddaughter. I hope you don't mind, but I sort of volunteered you to help them solve a sixty-year-old mystery."

Tony raised a brow. "Sixty years old?"

"Love found, love lost, questions lingering without any answers. I suppose that after all this time a few unanswered questions might not seem all that important, but I could sense they were important to the woman who had held them in her heart."

"I suppose you should start at the beginning."

I smiled. "It all started when a man met a woman and fell in love…"

Chapter 3

Monday, March 18

"Morning, Hap," I said to Hap Hollister, the owner of the local home-and-hardware store as Tilly and I entered through the front door to deliver his daily mail.

"Tess; Tilly. It looks like another beautiful day."

I smiled. "So beautiful. Rationally, I know that this is only March and we are likely to get more snow before summer actually arrives, but this springlike weather has definitely given me a case of spring fever. I actually had serious thoughts about getting out my deck furniture, but then I realized how crazy that would be when it is almost guaranteed that it will snow at least one more time."

"I've had two customers come in this morning looking for annuals for their barrels and baskets. I had to remind them that I wouldn't be stocking the delicate flowers until the middle of May, which is almost two months away. It's hard not to want to skip the next eight weeks and get right to it, but by the time you get to be my age, you realize that time, even time spent during the winter, is too precious to wish away."

I set a stack of mail on the counter. "I hear you. I suppose there are no guarantees at any age. I guess you heard about Brick."

Hap tightened his lips and bowed his head. "I heard. Such a damn shame. I just can't imagine who would want to kill a nice guy like him."

"Tony thinks it might have been a customer who had too much to drink and took out their anger and frustration on the only person around. I suppose it could have happened that way, especially if drugs were involved. But it is too early to know for sure. It could also have been someone with a grudge who came to the bar after it closed with the intention of killing him."

"Does Mike have a theory?" Hap asked.

"I haven't talked to him today, but as of yesterday around dinnertime, he had no idea what had happened or who might be guilty. He's a good cop; he'll figure it out. Do you have any outgoing mail?"

Hap reached under the counter and brought up a single manila envelope. "Just the one item today. Have you been by Hattie's yet?"

Hattie was Hap's ex-wife and current girlfriend. Or something like that. To be honest, I wasn't really clear on their current marital status. "Not yet. I started on the north end of the street today."

"When you see her, can you ask her to answer her dad-gum phone? I've been calling her all morning and it just rings through to her voice mail."

"I hope nothing is wrong."

Hap's lips tightened as he shook his head. "Nothing is wrong. We had a spat over the weekend and I'm willing to bet she is avoiding me. She made it clear that she was not going to speak to me until I apologized, but how is a man supposed to apologize if she won't answer her dang phone?"

I picked up Hap's envelope and slipped it into my bag. "I'm certainly not an expert when it comes to relationships and have made plenty of my own mistakes along the way, but it seems to me that if Hattie is mad enough to avoid you, an apology in person might be called for."

Hap groaned. "I was afraid of that. She knows I don't do well with the mushy stuff."

"An apology doesn't have to be mushy, it just has to be sincere."

After we left Hap's, Tilly and I continued south, crossing the street when we came to Sisters' Diner, the restaurant owned by my mother and my Aunt Ruthie. There was a thick envelope addressed to my mom with no return address that I will admit I was supercurious about. As a mail carrier, the things my customers received were considered to be confidential and absolutely none of my business, but as a daughter...

"Oh good, the best of dining magazine came," Aunt Ruthie said when I handed her their stack of mail. "I know we don't change up our menu all that much, but I do enjoy thumbing through to see what is new and what is over. It can be challenging to keep up with the latest fads, although our clientele is a bit different from the one you would encounter in a big city."

"Food fads?" I asked. "I never really thought about food as being something that went in and out of style."

"Do you remember fondue?"

"Yeah, I guess."

"Do you ever see fondue on a menu in any of the White Eagle restaurants nowadays?"

"No, I guess I don't. Seems like I don't see nearly as many wraps, skillet meals, or kabobs as I once did either."

"So you get what I am saying."

I nodded. "I do. So what's in now?"

Ruthie paused to consider my question. "In a way, it depends on your geography. I know that raw food, low carb, gluten free, and dairy free are popular trends in parts of the country, but here in White Eagle, I've noticed that a lot of customers have moved away from trendy entrées and begun to request traditional, home-style ones, much like the meals our grandparents served up on Sunday afternoons."

"So you are saying meat, potatoes, veggies, and home-baked rolls have replaced low carb and fat free?"

"For the most part. Of course, I also predict that this warm weather will cause people to start thinking about bathing suits and skimpy shorts, so I imagine that salads and low-carb items will be making a comeback."

I had a feeling that Ruthie was right about that. "I imagine you heard about Brick," I said, changing the subject.

Ruthie nodded. "Mike stopped by for breakfast. I just don't understand what this world is coming to.

For a man to be gunned down in his own place of business is reprehensible."

"I agree. Did Mike say if he had any leads?"

Ruthie shook her head. "No, he didn't. Though he did shoot out of here after receiving a text, despite the fact that he was only half done with his meal."

"Seems significant. I have to say I'm curious, but I have a job to do, so I'll have to put that on the back burner for now. Is Mom around?"

"She took a break so she could go to her garden club meeting."

"Garden club? It's March."

"It would appear this heat wave has put everyone in the mood for spring. The group usually doesn't meet between November and April, but I guess a few of the gals wanted to start talking seeds, so they decided to meet. It's been slow today, so it was fine with me if your mom wanted to take some time off."

Oh well, it looked as if my curiosity regarding the envelope Mom had received would have to wait. "Okay, then, I guess I will see you tomorrow. Have a wonderful rest of your day."

I decided to cross the road and continue on that side so as to arrive at Mike's office sooner rather than later. That would result in a circle eight sort of delivery pattern, which might confuse some of the business owners who might have been anticipating my arrival, but I wanted to see what, if anything, Mike might have discovered since the evening before. It was possible he might not even be in his office with an active investigation underway, but I supposed if he wasn't, I could always swing back by once my route was done.

"Morning, Frank," I greeted Mike's partner. "Mike in?"

"No. He's out talking to folks about what happened over at Brick's place. I'm holding down the fort here."

"Have you heard anything?" I set a pile of mail on Frank's desk, then slipped off my mailbag and sat down on the chair across the desk from him. Tilly wandered over to say hi to Mike's dog, Leonard, who had been sleeping next to Frank's chair.

"A couple of folks have mentioned that Brick was spotted having an argument with Lance Castle on Saturday night," Frank answered. "It seems it was a pretty lively discussion regarding Lance's assertion that Brick had been stepping out with his wife. Those who overheard it tended to agree that Lance was drunk and not making a lot of sense. Brick kicked him out, but there are some folks who suspected he might have come back to the bar after closing to settle the argument once and for all."

I knew Lance. He was a hothead who liked to spout off about things he knew nothing about, seemingly just to make noise. He was a hunter and he had at least one gun that I knew of. "What sort of gun was used to kill Brick?"

"We don't have the bullet, but it looks like he was shot with a handgun at fairly close range."

"You don't have the slug? Where is it?"

"It looks like the killer dug it out of the wall and took it with him."

That didn't strike me as the action of a man who was drunk out of his mind. It sounded a lot more like a man, or a woman, who showed up with a clear head and murder on their mind.

"What did Lance say when he was asked about his whereabouts on Saturday night?"

"He admitted to getting skunk drunk before going to the bar, where he confronted Brick about having an affair with his wife. He said he didn't remember Brick kicking him out, but that fit the fact that he woke up slumped over the wheel of his car, which, apparently, he ran off the road and into a field shortly after leaving the bar. He said he didn't remember what happened between the time he confronted Brick and when he woke up in his car, but he did say that he was sure he hadn't shot Brick. The lack of either a gun in his car or gunshot residue on his hands or clothing seems to confirm that, but it is possible he is lying."

"But if he was lying about shooting Brick, wouldn't he have residue on his hands and clothes?"

"Not if he shot Brick, went home and took a shower and cleaned up, then drove his car into the field, where he waited until morning so he'd have an alibi."

"If he had the presence of mind to actually plan an alibi, the one he came up with seems pretty lame."

Frank shrugged. "Maybe. All we can do at this point is dig up every lead we can and then follow the evidence, or lack of evidence, to its natural conclusion."

"I guess that much is true. Are there any other suspects right now?"

"A few. I know that Mike planned to talk to Lance's wife and his best friend today, so maybe he either will have cleared or arrested Lance by the time you come back here. If Lance turns out to be innocent, though, my money is on Dover Boswell."

Dover Boswell was one of Brick's part-time bartenders. "Why do you suspect him?"

"Brick fired him a couple of weeks ago."

"Why? He seems like a nice guy."

"Brick accused him of stealing. He even came in here and tried to get us to arrest him, but Brick didn't have any evidence to back up his claim. I did speak to Dover afterward, and he claimed he was innocent. I will say that the guy was about as mad as I've ever seen him. I suppose being madder than a wet hen doesn't mean that he was mad enough to kill the guy. For all I know, Dover might be guilty of stealing from Brick, as he insisted he was. I know both men fairly well, and Dover doesn't strike me as the sort to steal from his boss, but then, Brick didn't strike me as the sort to make up lies either. I just hope that Dover doesn't get pulled into this if he is innocent. He has a wife and two little kids to think about."

"And if he isn't innocent?"

"If he did steal from Brick, and especially if he killed him, then of course he needs to pay for what he's done."

I glanced at the clock on the wall. "As interested as I am in this case, I need to finish my route. I might come back at the end of the day to talk to Mike if he is around."

I left the police station with a lot on my mind. Dover Boswell? I just couldn't see it. He seemed like such a nice guy. I honestly couldn't imagine him as a thief *or* a killer. Lance Castle, on the other hand... The more I thought about it, the more I realized that I could totally see him as the sort of person who would kill someone.

Deciding that if I wanted to get my route done before the businesses in town closed for the day I needed to get going, I put all thoughts of murder out of my mind and focused on the task before me. My next stop was the furniture store, followed by the five-and-dime. Both would be easy to get in and out of, but after that was the Book Boutique, Bree's store, and my stop there always demanded at least a fifteen-minute conversation.

"I only have a few minutes," I said to her the minute I walked in to the bookstore. "Everyone wants to talk about Brick's murder, which has put me way behind schedule."

"Is there any news?" Bree asked as I handed her a stack of mail.

"Not really. There is a lot of speculation, but I don't think anyone really knows what happened. Did Mike come back by your place after he got off last night?"

"No. He texted to let me know he would be working late, so he was going to go straight home. I'm hoping that he won't have to work late tonight too. I really need to talk to him about The Lakehouse as a venue for the wedding."

"Maybe you can arrange to meet for dinner even if he does have to work late. I know you hoped he could go with you to tour the facility, but if he can't take the time off to do it, I suppose you can just ask him for his opinion and then take the tour yourself. Or I can go with you, if you don't want to go alone. It's not like you and Mike haven't been there before. You know what the place looks like, so all you really need to do is to meet with the event coordinator to discuss the specifics of your particular affair."

Bree set her mail on the counter. "I guess that could work. I'll call Mike later to see what his day looks like. If I need you to go with me, I'll text you. I might even be able to convince the woman I spoke to yesterday to give us more time to commit once I explain the situation. I really want Mike to be part of this decision."

"I know you do. And I'm sure he wants that as well. I need to run, but I'll call you later and we can chat more about it."

"Thanks, Tess. Oh, by the way, I wanted to ask if you'd stopped by Sue's Sewing Nook yet."

"No, not yet. I'm doing a circle-eight route today."

"The book she ordered came in. Do you think you can drop it off when you bring her her mail?"

"Yeah, I can do that. Do you have it handy?"

Bree reached under the counter and handed me the package. "Thanks. I could have called her and asked her to come by to pick it up herself, but it is already paid for, so this will save her a trip."

"No problem. I am always happy to help out when I can."

I said my goodbyes and went back out into the sunshine. Tilly and I had managed to get 90 percent of our route done when I received a text from Tony letting me know he had news about Elizabeth Bradford's missing fiancé and wondering if I wanted to grab dinner later. I texted back that I would meet him at my cabin as soon as I finished my route. He offered to get there early to make us dinner, which sounded even better to me.

Chapter 4

By the time Tilly and I got home, Tony had something that smelled wonderful in the oven. I greeted Titan and then kissed Tony hello. My cats, Tang and Tinder, were sitting on the sofa watching my progress, but neither went to the effort of getting up to say hi.

"The chicken-and-penne casserole will be ready in about fifteen minutes if you want to change out of your uniform and get comfortable."

"Is this your chicken and penne with the creamy Cajun seasoning?" I asked, taking a deep breath of the spicy scent.

"It is. I have rosemary bread and salad as well. Oh, and I ran into Mike when I was in town picking up supplies for dinner. He said to call him when you get a chance."

"Did he say what about?"

"He just said he had a question for you about Brick's mail last week."

Brick's mail? Now that could be interesting. I tried to think back as I changed into a pair of jeans and a pale blue sweatshirt. The bar didn't get a lot of mail. In fact, if he got mail two days in the same week, I'd say it was a busy one for him, and it wasn't unheard of for him to go three or four weeks in a row without receiving anything but junk mail. And he almost never passed any outgoing mail to me. I supposed he just dropped off his mail at the post office rather than hanging on to it for me to take. A lot of people did. I played through the previous week in my mind. I was pretty sure Brick hadn't had any mail on Monday, but he had received a couple of items on Tuesday. An official-looking letter with a logo in the top left-hand corner with a typewritten address in the center of the envelope, alerting the post office that it was to go to Brick at the bar. On the same day he'd received that businesslike letter, he had also received a larger envelope, which might have contained a document of some sort. A signature indicating proof of delivery was requested for that second item, which also had been professionally addressed and, if I remembered correctly, it had the same logo as the return address as the smaller letter. Brick didn't have outgoing mail for me to take on Tuesday, and he neither sent nor received mail on Wednesday, but on Thursday he received a large envelope that felt like it could contain a magazine or a catalog, but, now that I thought about it, might have held additional documents, and an envelope with a handwritten address that looked like a letter or other personal correspondence. The handwritten envelope didn't have a return address, but I had noticed that the postmark was from Iowa.

You might wonder how I could remember such details, and the simple answer is that Brick received mail that was not just a flyer or a solicitation of some sort so rarely that his mail, when it was something of substance, tended to stand out in my mind. Plus, I will admit that delivering the mail could become routine, so I tended to notice what sorts of things customers I knew well received.

After I changed, I used my cell to call Mike. As anticipated, his question had to do with items that might have been delivered by myself or some other delivery service. Mike was interested to know if I had delivered a box to Brick during the week prior to his death. I informed him that I had not. I asked about the presence of a tracking number or some other sort of delivery service indicator, and he told me that the postmark had indicated that the box had been sent via the United States Postal Service. Okay, that was weird. If Brick had received a box, I, as his mail carrier, would have been the one to deliver it. Unless, of course, it was too large or too heavy. I asked Mike about the size and weight, and he informed me that the box was a cube of about one foot in length, width, and depth. It was empty now, so he was unable to ascertain its weight when mailed, but from the charge to mail the darn thing, he imagined that whatever was in the box must have weighed about five pounds.

I assured Mike that I had not seen or delivered the box, and he said that he was going to check with some of the other folks who worked at the local branch of the post office.

I went downstairs for dinner as soon as I hung up the phone.

"Did you have the information Mike was looking for?" Tony asked after I slid onto a stool at the counter so we could chat while he finished preparing our meal.

"No. He was looking for information regarding the delivery of a box he found at Brick's place. He said it had a USPS label on it, but I'm pretty sure I've never delivered a box to Brick. He did receive mail last week, though, which was odd in its own right."

Tony opened the oven and pulled out a casserole dish with cheese bubbling on the top of it. "Brick didn't normally receive mail?"

I shook my head. "Rarely. And he almost never received mail twice in one week, other than junk mail, of course. Last week he received four items in all. Two on Tuesday and two on Thursday."

Tony picked up a salad bowl and headed toward the dining table. "Did Mike seem to think that any of the items he received might be relevant?"

I frowned. "He didn't ask for a description of the items and I didn't provide one. The entire conversation was actually pretty quick."

Tony set a basket of bread on the table and then handed me a plate so that I could serve myself a portion of the casserole, which was cooling on a hot pad placed on the kitchen counter. "Do you think any of the mail Brick received might reveal something about his murder?"

I paused before answering. I scooped up a large spoonful of casserole and then carried it to the table. "Maybe. On Tuesday he received formal-looking correspondence in a business-letter-size envelope. There was even a logo where the return address would usually go."

"Did you notice the identity of the sender?"

"No. I had no way of knowing what was going to happen, so I didn't pay all that much attention to the logo other than to notice it was there."

Tony sat down across from me. I picked up my glass and took a sip of my water.

"Anything else on Tuesday?" he asked.

"A larger envelope that looked and felt like it might be a document of some sort. And no, I didn't notice the return address on that one either, though I'm pretty sure it also had a logo where the return address would be." I went on to tell Tony about the two items that I delivered on Thursday.

"So, we have a business-letter-size envelope with a typed address and logo, something that felt like loose pages or a document, a package that felt as if it had a magazine or catalog within, and a letter-size item with a handwritten address."

I nodded. "That sounds right."

Tony took a bite of his casserole. "I wonder if any or all of the items you delivered are still in the bar."

I shrugged. "I don't know. I guess we can look."

"The bar is closed," Tony pointed out.

"I suppose I can call Mike again."

"That might be a good idea. Just because he didn't ask about Brick's mail delivery other than the box doesn't mean he shouldn't know about the mail."

I grabbed a second piece of bread from the basket. "When you called earlier, you mentioned that you had news about the case of the missing fiancé."

"I do. Well, I don't have news exactly, but a lack of evidence to support our theory is something, I suppose."

"Okay, then, what didn't you find?"

"Anything relating to a man named Patrick O'Malley living in Boston who would have been twenty-four in 1959."

"Did you widen your search to include a larger geographic area as well as maybe a slightly wider age range?"

Tony nodded. "From the information I could find—which, keep in mind, was not at all as readily available back then as it is now—there were seven men named Patrick O'Malley between the ages of twenty-two and twenty-six living in Boston or its suburbs in 1959. If you throw in hyphenated names such as Patrick-Michael or John-Patrick, there were sixteen men who fit the profile."

"Don't you think someone named John-Patrick would go by John, not Patrick?"

"Not if his father's name was also John-Patrick, and the father went by John."

He had a point. "Are any of these men still alive?"

"I haven't gotten that far yet. It occurred to me that we are going to need more information if we are going to narrow things down."

"Why don't you cross-reference Patrick using all the criteria you used for the last search but add in an association with Toby Willis, the man Elizabeth Bradford told Jennifer Anne was with the group Patrick accompanied to White Eagle. She said he was about the same age as Patrick."

Tony smiled. "That is a very good idea. I'll see what I can turn up."

As soon as we finished eating, Tony cleaned up the kitchen while I called Mike and asked about the location of the mail I had delivered to Brick last week. I had no way of knowing if any of it played into Brick's murder, but I figured it couldn't hurt to bring it up. He responded by telling me that Brick had left piles of mail on his desk in the bar, and if I thought the mail I'd delivered the week before his death could be important, I could meet him there in an hour. He hoped I would be able to identify the four envelopes in question.

******

Mike was already inside the bar when Tony and I arrived. He'd left the door open, so we let ourselves in. I could see a light that must originate from Brick's office, which was located at the end of a hallway that also led to both the men's and women's restrooms, as well as a large storage room.

"I think this might be every piece of correspondence I've delivered to Brick since he purchased this place." I picked up a handful of envelopes from the desk. Many of them were empty. I had to wonder why Brick hadn't shredded them, or at least tossed them in the bin.

"Do you recognize the envelopes you dropped off last week?" Mike asked.

I picked up the large envelope that I'd thought might contain a magazine or catalog. It was empty, but the postmark confirmed that it was the item I had delivered on Thursday. There was no return address, so I wasn't sure how I could ever determine what was inside the envelope when I dropped it by. The other envelope I dropped off on Tuesday was also in the pile. There was a logo from a company called Genocom where the return address should be, but like the first envelope, it was empty. I sorted through the entirety of the contents on Brick's desk, but I wasn't able to locate either the envelope with the handwritten address or the letter-size envelope with the typewritten address.

"I suppose he may have taken the two smaller items home with him," Tony said.

"I guess it wouldn't hurt to head over to his house to take a look," Mike said. "Any idea what sort of company Genocom is?"

"I've heard of them," Tony said. "They specialize in genetics, researching genetically transmitted diseases and disorders, and are actively looking for ways to both prevent and cure those sorts of abnormalities. They also are involved in some of the more controversial types of research dealing with cloning and cell manipulation."

"Why would Brick be in to any of that?" I asked.

"He might have been after something as simple as a DNA profile, which the company also provides for those who are willing to pay for it."

"You mean they do DNA profiles like those internet companies that have you spit into a container and allow you to find out the basics of your genetic makeup?" Mike asked.

"They do offer that service, but they also do DNA profiling that is much more specific. For example, if you wanted to test the likelihood that two people are related, they would be able to give you information about that. Or if you found DNA at the scene of a crime and wanted to compare it with the DNA of a suspect, they could do that as well."

"So maybe Brick was searching for his roots," I said.

Tony shrugged. "Perhaps. If we want to know for sure why Brick contacted this company, you will either need to find the correspondence he received from them, or Mike will need to get a search warrant to access his file at Genocom."

"Looking for the pages that were in the envelope seems the path of least resistance," Mike said.

I nodded. "Let's go over to Brick's house to see what we can find."

Brick lived in a modest, one-bedroom home not far from the bar. It wasn't exactly a health hazard, but it was a mess, and I really didn't understand why anyone would choose to live like that. As with his office at the bar, he had one surface—in this case, a table—piled high with old magazines, mail, and receipts. Luckily, the letter-size piece of correspondence I had delivered on Tuesday was right on top. Like the larger envelope we'd found in the bar, it featured a Genocom logo where the return address would usually be. I opened the envelope to find a sheet of paper letting Brick know that the information he'd asked for had been sent in a separate envelope because he'd chosen hard copies rather than email documents, and the receipt for the work he'd commissioned was included in the envelope as well.

"Seems like we need to find whatever was in that envelope," Mike said.

"It'll be tough because we don't know what we are looking for," I responded.

"If Brick ordered genetic testing of some sort, the report would most likely contain graphs as well as text," Tony offered. He picked up a pile of paperwork and mail from the table. "I guess we start sorting."

"Look for a letter-size envelope with a handwritten address and a postmark that would indicate it was mailed last week too," I said.

Tony, Mike, and I continued to look through the stack for at least thirty minutes before Mike tossed the things he'd been working on onto the rest. "If the report or whatever it was that Genocom sent Brick were here, I would think it would be right on the top."

"If the information was damaging in some way, it is possible that Brick would secure the report so it wouldn't be easily found," Mike pointed out.

I stood up and stretched my back. "Did anyone notice a safe in the bar office?" I asked.

"No," Tony answered, "but we weren't looking for one, and it does make sense that he would have one. Brick pulled in a lot of cash between five o'clock on Friday, when the banks close, and eight a.m. on Monday, when they open. It makes sense that he'd have a safe to store it in."

Tony was right. It made sense that Brick would have a safe somewhere in the bar. "Should we look around here first? It's a small place, but I suppose we shouldn't assume that Brick didn't have a safe for personal use here."

"Okay, let's look around," Mike said. "Be sure to look behind every picture, look behind the clothes in every closet, and look for loose floorboards. Think like a thief. That's what I do when I am trying to figure out where someone might have stashed something."

A thorough search of the house netted us zero results, so we piled back into our cars and drove back toward the bar.

"Has Brick ever mentioned family members to you?" Tony asked.

I paused to consider. "No, not that I can remember. I don't think he has any family in town. He hasn't been married since I've known him, and I don't remember him ever mentioning having children." I let my mind wander back. "There was one man. An uncle, I think." I focused harder. "I remember delivering a letter to him just before we headed out of town for Thanksgiving. Brick said the letter was from his uncle, who lived out of town and planned a visit. He said he wasn't sure exactly when he was coming because the man's plans were pretty loose and open. He wondered if the uncle would be in town on Thanksgiving and if he would be expected to cook." I looked at Tony. "I suggested a precooked meal."

"Do you remember mentioning a name?"

I tapped my finger on my chin. "No. Jordan Westlake walked into the bar right at about that time, and I changed the subject because I wanted to ask him about his visit with the Harrington twins. I never got back to talking with Brick about his uncle."

"I suppose it would be easy to use Brick as a starting point to look for possible family members. Maybe he had the scoop on the unknown parentage of one of his cousins, or perhaps he wondered if his uncle was actually his father."

"I guess that is the sort of thing one might go to Genocom to find out."

Tony pulled into the bar's parking lot behind Mike. We parked and got out, then followed Mike inside and down the hallway to Brick's office. It made the most sense that if he had a safe, that would be where we'd find it. Eventually, we found a floor safe under the area rug. Of course, as any safe would be, it was locked.

"Can't you just break it open?" I asked.

"Not without a search warrant," Mike said. "I should be able to get one pretty quickly, given the nature of our investigation. I want to thank you both for helping. I'll call you tomorrow to let you know what I find."

Well, that was anticlimactic. The fact that we'd seemingly come so close but still didn't know what had been going on in Brick's life immediately before his death left me feeling itchy and unsatisfied. The wait was, of course, understandably necessary. This was an official investigation, and anything Mike found couldn't be used in a court of law unless he followed proper protocol.

Tony and I drove back to my cabin while Mike headed out to meet Bree. As far as I knew, they hadn't made it to The Lakehouse yet, but Bree hadn't called for my help, so maybe she had convinced the woman in charge of leasing to give her more time.

"I know this is Mike's case, but I wonder if we should do our own background search. Just to find out things like whether Brick has living relatives besides his uncle, or who we might contact to obtain additional information."

"It is Mike's case. He's a cop. He is perfectly qualified to do a background search and obtain that information," Tony reminded me. "If he asks for help, I will absolutely provide it, but we did agree to take a step back and let him do his job."

I let out a long, slow breath. "Yeah, I know. I just feel sort of antsy. Like we should be doing something."

Tony leaned over and kissed me gently on the lips. "I can think of a few things to fill our time."

I smiled. "Yeah. Like what?"

Tony whispered in my ear.

I wasn't sure what I was expecting, but it wasn't a challenge to try to best him in the new video game he was helping his best friend, Shaggy, test.

I raised a brow. "You have it? Here with you right now?"

Tony nodded.

I couldn't help but grin. Gaming with Tony was one of my favorite things to do. It was, among other things, the link that had made us friends in the first place. "Game on, puny mortal; game on."

Chapter 5

Tuesday, March 19

Mike was able to get a search warrant to open Brick's safe easily enough. It turned out to contain a whole lot of money and a thirty-page document, complete with graphs, charts, and details relating to the genetic makeup of four individuals. The problem was, all of the names had been replaced with letters, making it impossible to know whose DNA Brick had had tested. Despite having the information, we didn't know why Brick wanted it.

"This report looks different," I said, holding up several sheets of paper labeled *Subject K*. "The results aren't the same. It almost looks like the K results are much older. There is a lot less information provided, and the documents have a different look to them."

Mike took a closer look at the report for subject K. "This looks like a request for DNA testing from a lab in Des Moines, Iowa. And you're right, it isn't all that recent."

"Can I take a look?" Tony asked.

Mike handed him the report.

Tony took a closer look. "It appears that subject K and subject L are the same person."

"Okay, that is weird. Right?" I asked, petting Tilly distractedly on the top of the head.

"It appears as if the document relating to subject K is the document that Brick was testing the other DNA samples against. Maybe the results for K are for some other person Brick wanted to identify."

I frowned. "I don't understand."

"Perhaps K is someone known to Brick by relationship only," Tony explained. "For example, maybe Brick never knew his father, but he had his DNA profile for some reason. I will admit that would be odd, but bear with me on this for now. Maybe Brick suspected four men of being his father based on what his mother had told him, and he wanted to know which of them he was actually related to, so he took DNA samples from all four and had them tested against the original sample."

"So we are looking at a twist on a *Mamma Mia!* thing?" I asked.

Tony shrugged. "I don't know for sure, but it is an explanation that can be used to demonstrate a possible scenario. I'm sure there are others."

Mike picked up the report from subject K. "This report is not part of the report from Genocom describing the genetic makeup of subjects B, S, L, or A. We aren't close to figuring out why Brick was doing this testing, but it seems that whatever Brick was doing was important to him. I bet reports with this amount of detail don't come cheap."

"So the real question is, what was Brick looking in to, and was that what got him killed?" Tony asked.

"We know that the letter with the typewritten address was from Genocom and the large envelope with the logo was most likely the report for subjects B, S, L, and A, and we suspect the other large envelope might have been the report relating to subject K, which is different from the others, but what about the other letter?" I asked. "The one with the handwritten address. Is that in the safe as well?"

Mike shook his head. "No, I'm afraid not."

"What are the odds that we can get a court order to gain access to the names behind the four samples that were tested at Genocom?" Tony asked.

"If we can come up with compelling evidence that the tests that Brick commissioned from Genocom are directly related to his murder, we may be able to get a court order demanding that the company provide us with that information, but short of that, the confidentiality between the company and the client will probably prevail. After we found the first letter, I called Genocom and spoke to a clerk who wouldn't give me squat. I guess I can try speaking to someone higher up in the hierarchy of the company. Perhaps I can get them to cooperate voluntarily."

"It's worth a try." I began walking around the small room. It was dusty and cluttered, and I wasn't sure how Brick had gotten any work done in here. I really wanted to find the handwritten letter. In my mind, it could very well be the key to making sense of the murder. I began opening and closing the cabinet doors of the built-ins that lined one wall. The contents didn't seem to be arranged in any sort of logical order. There was a packing slip from a recent alcohol order on the same shelf as an old beer tap, a leather wristband with several handstamped symbols on it, a box of toothpicks, and a pack of chewing gum that must have long since gone stale.

"Have you checked out Brick's computer?" I asked Mike. I'd noticed that it was missing from the desk, where I'd seen it on a previous visit.

"We haven't been able to find it. I know Brick had just one laptop for both business and personal use, so when we didn't find it on his desk during our initial search of the bar, I just figured it was in his car or at home, but we haven't been able to locate it in either location."

"What about his cell?" Tony asked.

"It was in his pocket when he was shot. We have it down at the station. It is password protected, and so far, we haven't been able to access it."

I looked around the office in search of a clue. Besides the furniture, there were photos, awards, and certificates on the walls, dusty books on the shelves, a couple of bowling trophies, and a whole lot of clutter. I noticed a half-full glass of whiskey on the credenza in the back of the room "Did anyone think to dust that glass for prints?"

Mike frowned. "I don't remember seeing it there when I was here before."

I thought about our visit the previous day. I hadn't noticed the glass then either, but then, I hadn't been looking for it. Chances were Brick had been enjoying a whiskey while he cleaned up on Saturday night. He could have come back to the office to finish up some paperwork or to store the cash taken that evening in the safe. Maybe he'd heard a noise, set the glass down while he went to investigate, and then was shot before he could return to the office. Or perhaps, I amended, someone had broken in and helped themselves to a drink.

"I'll take the glass back to the station with me," Mike stated.

"I think we should keep our eyes open for other correspondence that might have something to do with the report from Genocom, and maybe we should dig into Brick's family tree," I suggested. "If we can find a child he never knew about but had recently surfaced, or a parent who abandoned him as a child and he decided to track down, that could explain the Genocom tests." I looked at Mike. "This part of the story began with a box you found that appeared to have been carried and delivered by the USPS but never came through my hands. Were you ever able to figure out who did deliver it? I meant to ask around this morning, but I was late to work and the other mail carriers had already headed out on their routes."

"I did inquire about the box. None of the other carriers admitted to having delivered it, yet that nice woman at the desk was able to confirm it had been checked in at the sorting station in Missoula and was dropped off at this post office a week ago Friday for delivery the following Monday."

"So someone who has access to the back room of the post office must have seen the package and taken it to Brick before it was assigned to a carrier."

Mike nodded. "That would be my guess."

"The only reason I can come up with for someone doing it is that whatever was in the box was time sensitive and Brick somehow managed to convince someone with access to the back room to fetch the box for him rather than making him wait until

Monday. While not kosher, bypassing a carrier is not unheard of. I wonder why whoever took the box and gave it to Brick doesn't simply own up to having done so."

Mike shrugged. "Your guess is as good as mine."

I glanced at my watch. Tilly and I needed to get back out. "I'll call you this evening to touch base," I said as I started to walk away. "Oh, I meant to ask, did Bree talk to you about going with her to look at The Lakehouse?"

Mike nodded. "She did. We are meeting the event coordinator there at five. And Tess, thanks for helping her to work out a doable compromise."

"That's what the maid of honor is supposed to do."

By the time I returned to my route, I was a good thirty minutes behind schedule. I'd need to hurry to get caught up, so I tried very hard to just deliver the mail without stopping to talk to everyone. Of course, executing a drop-and-run was not always easy, especially when everyone had questions about Brick and White Eagle's latest murder investigation. Still, I was able to set a good pace until I arrived at Sue's Sewing Nook. Sue was a lifelong town resident, as was I, and as a lifelong resident who was also a descendent of Dillinger Wade, one of White Eagle's founding fathers, she took news as horrifying as a murder in the community very seriously.

"I was hoping you'd be by while I was between customers," Sue said when I entered her cute and eclectic shop. "I'm dying to find out what you know about Brick's murder."

"Not a lot." I set a stack of mail on the counter next to the cash register. "If you take into account the drunken shooter angle, there are a host of suspects to consider."

"Do you think that is what happened?" Sue asked. "Do you think some random drunk killed Brick?"

I shrugged. "I don't know. Mike doesn't know. I don't think anyone knows yet." I turned to make a quick exit but then paused. "I know this is a personal question and you don't have to answer it if you don't want to, but it just occurred to me that I delivered an envelope to you maybe six months ago with the same logo on the upper left-hand corner as a letter I delivered to Brick the week before he died."

"Oh? And what logo was that?"

"It belonged to a company called Genocom."

Sue smiled. "Your memory is correct. In fact, I was the one who told Brick about the company. He had some DNA he wanted tested and I'd used them when I found out about Austin and was happy with the results."

"I wasn't aware that Austin planned to tell the entire family about the facts surrounding his birth," I said, remembering back to the murder investigation that revealed that Austin Wade, the head of the family, wasn't a Wade by birth.

"He wasn't, but when the truth came out, he decided to come clean with everyone. Austin kept the secret for a long time, but in the end, I think he was happy to clear the air."

"I see. And whose DNA did you test?"

"My own, of course. I wanted to be certain that I was actually who I believed myself to be, which, of course, I am. No hidden controversy here."

I supposed I could understand her concern. "Do you know whose DNA Brick wanted to test?" I asked.

Sue shook her head. "I didn't ask. I figured that he would tell me if he wanted me to know, and he didn't, so I let it go."

I was about to ask about the method of DNA collection Genocom used when a customer walked in. I really wanted to continue our conversation, but I also wanted to get my route done in time. I figured my questions could wait, so I waved goodbye to Sue and continued on my way.

When I arrived at Bree's bookstore, there was a sign in the window letting customers know she would be closed that afternoon. Weird. I supposed she might not have felt well, or perhaps she was busy with wedding plans. I decided to just hang on to her mail and deliver it to her home later in the day. If she was hung up and we weren't able to connect, I could always give her today's mail tomorrow. I continued on my way and was able to make good time on the next dozen deliveries. I arrived at Sisters' Diner after closing, but I saw Mom and Aunt Ruthie through the window, still inside cleaning up, so I used my key and entered the restaurant.

"There she is," Mom said. "We thought you'd skipped us today."

"I was just behind after spending time with Mike and have been playing catch-up all day." I handed my mom a stack of mail.

"I was hoping that Mike or Frank would pop in for lunch so I could ask them about Brick's murder investigation, but I haven't seen either of them all day," Aunt Ruthie complained.

"I think they are both pretty busy," I answered. "It's a tough case. No one seems to have seen anything, and while there are a bunch of possible motives for the shooting, I don't think either Mike or Frank have been able to come up with the real one yet."

"Most folks are speculating that Brick was killed during a robbery," Mom said.

"I guess that is possible. He did have a lot of money in his safe. If he was killed in the course of a robbery, though, the killer didn't get what he was looking for. When Mike opened the safe, there was all sorts of cash just sitting there."

"What if the killer was after something other than money?" Ruthie asked.

"Something like what?" I wondered.

"I overheard a group of folks from the senior center saying that they'd heard that Brick was selling illegal drugs out of the bar."

I wrinkled my nose. "Drugs? That doesn't seem like Brick."

"I agree." Ruthie nodded. "Still, folks are talking, and that is just one of the things I've heard. Leo from over at the filling station and minimart has been saying that Brick was secretive and moody lately, which seems to support the idea that he may have been not only selling drugs but taking them too."

"I wasn't aware that Brick and Leo were friends."

"As far as I know, they aren't. Leo said that Brick got his gas there sometimes. I imagine they chatted when Brick went in to pay."

I couldn't help but roll my eyes. This was how rumors got started: a man who spent a minute chatting with Brick maybe twice a month had the impression that he was moody and withdrawn, and suddenly he was a drug addict. "I'm sure Mike did a tox screen. He didn't mention anything about drugs to me."

"Maybe he doesn't have the results yet. Those things can take time."

"Or maybe Leo doesn't know what he's talking about." I let out a breath. "I get the idea that everyone is anxious to understand what led to Brick's death, but I think that spreading around rumors based on nothing more than pure conjecture can be damaging both to Mike's investigation and Brick's reputation."

Ruthie lifted a shoulder. "I guess you might have a point. Leo doesn't strike me as the sort to know much about anything, yet he does always seem to have an opinion."

I turned toward my mother. "So, how was your garden club yesterday?"

As I suspected it would, her expression showed momentary confusion, which she quickly masked with a smile.

"It was lovely. It is a little early in the year for us to meet, but with the warm weather, everyone was feeling ambitious. It is still much too soon to plant, but I enjoyed having a chance to catch up with everyone."

"I just spoke to Sue a few minutes ago, and she didn't say anything about a meeting."

Mom shrugged. "Only a few of us met. I wouldn't even call it a garden club meeting. It was more like lunch with friends. Did I hear that you'd managed to convince Bree to have her wedding at an earlier time?"

"She, along with Mike, are meeting with the event coordinator at The Lakehouse. I think it is important for Bree to have the wedding she wants so she doesn't look back on her special day and find it lacking. But we have discussed options, and she seems okay with exploring a few other ideas. I should get going."

"Dinner on Sunday?" Mom called after me.

"I'll check with Tony and let you know."

Chapter 6

By the time I got home, Tony was there waiting for me. I was always happy when he was between projects because that meant he had time to focus on us. He'd just completed a huge job that he'd been working on since January for a German client and had assured me that he was going to be home in White Eagle for the foreseeable future.

"What's all this?" I asked after hanging up my jacket. The entire kitchen table was covered with what looked like blueprints.

"Plans for your patio garden."

I raised a brow. "My patio garden? I don't have a patio garden."

"I know, but last summer you admired mine, so I thought I'd build one for you as well."

I ran my hand over a sketch. "It's beautiful, but I don't have time to tend to a garden, patio or otherwise. Your garden really is spectacular, and I love the fact that you have fresh herbs and vegetables to cook with, but you are home during the day, at least when you are in town. I, on the other hand, work five days a week. If you add in my time at the animal shelter and at your place, I think you will see that I am not here much."

Tony lifted the lid of a pan and gave the contents a stir. "I guess you have a point. It does seem that you spend more time at my place in the summer than you do in the winter."

"That is because the commute into work is much easier without the snow to deal with. Plus, you have a lake and a hot tub that can be enjoyed under the stars. It really is a little piece of heaven."

Tony opened the oven door and took a peek inside. "Okay, message received. How about a hammock, a firepit, and a small water feature for your deck instead? Low maintenance but very cozy."

I smiled. "That sounds nice. Whatever you are making for dinner smells wonderful. I'm going to run upstairs and change out of my uniform. Can you feed Tilly? She is usually pretty hungry by the time we get done with our route."

"I'll take care of all the animals. Dinner won't be ready for thirty minutes, so take your time. I'll pick out a bottle of wine."

Who would have thought that Tess Thomas would end up with not only the perfect boyfriend but her own personal chef?

After I washed up and changed into comfy sweats, I joined Tony and the animals downstairs. The blueprints were gone and the table was set. Tony had made a fire and the dogs and cats were curled up in front of it. I was going to offer to help Tony in the kitchen, but he seemed to have everything under control, so I accepted a glass of wine and curled up on the sofa in front of the fire too.

"I spoke to Shaggy today," Tony said when he joined me on the sofa.

"And what has he been up to?"

"He has an idea for a video game he wants me to work on with him."

I turned and looked at Tony. "In other words, he wants you to do all the work."

Tony shook his head. "Not at all. Shaggy came up with the concept. He owns a video store and attends all the video game conventions, so he has an in when it comes time to market it. It is true that he will be looking to me for coding and funding, but I looked at his proposal and I think it is a good one. It has the potential to make us both a lot of money, but even if it doesn't, it will provide me with a change of pace from the financial and security software I usually deal with. Besides, it will provide me with something to do right here in White Eagle, which will mean no traveling for the next six months."

I smiled. "Well, that part sounds good. I know I give Shaggy a hard time because he usually acts like a twelve-year-old, but you know I like him, and the two of you have fun together. I think if this is a project you are excited about and you feel like you can afford to take the risk, you should go for it."

Tony grinned in return. "I just might. Shaggy's game is really different, which is not an easy thing to come up with in this day and age. I really think it will be a hit. Lord knows Shaggy and I have tested and offered feedback on enough prototypes that we have a feel for what will sell and what will flop. Our working together shouldn't affect you too much, except for the fact that I will need to be home on my computers more often and Shaggy will be hanging around even more than he does now."

"I like Shaggy just fine and don't have a problem with him hanging around, and I think the worst of the snow is behind us. I'm fine with schlepping my stuff out to your place rather than you coming here during the week."

"Maybe we should discuss bringing the cats out to my place on a temporary full-time basis so you don't have to crate them back and forth all the time. And I can clear out additional closet space so you can bring more of your clothes over."

"Works for me. If a storm blows in, I can always stay here for a few days if I need to."

Tony pulled out his phone. "Great. I'll text Shaggy to tell him we're on." He logged in, entered his password, and frowned.

"What is it?" I asked.

"I have an alert."

I sat up straighter. The last time he'd told me he had an alert was when his facial identification program had located my dad. "What kind of alert?"

"According to this, my program tagged a photo of your dad at a truck stop in Billings."

"Billings, Montana?"

Tony nodded.

I stood up, crossed the room, and held out my hand. "Let me see."

Tony handed me his phone. The man in the truck stop café was definitely my dad. He looked older than he had the last time I'd seen him. There was gray in his beard and his face showed the first lines, especially near his eyes. He was sitting at a table with another man who looked to be about his same age. I didn't think I'd ever met him, but he had the look of the other truckers I'd met over the years, who tended to be somewhat worn around the edges.

"I can't believe my dad is in Montana." Most of the other hits we'd received had been images captured at some point in the past. The only other real-time hit Tony had captured had been from a location in Eastern Europe. "I wonder why he is here."

"I have no idea." Tony looked at me. "I know we discussed ending our search for your dad. And I really haven't worked on it at all since our trip at Thanksgiving. But I didn't turn off this program, which has been running in the background. I can either turn it off now and we can forget we saw this photo, or I can increase the parameters and try to narrow in on where he will go next."

I hesitated. After pretty much confirming what I already suspected—that my father was in witness protection and had faked his own death to protect his family—I had all but decided to give up the search. There were those who knew more than I who had tried to convince me that letting it go, ending my search for answers, would be what my father would have wanted. But to have him this close…to know that with a few more hits we might be able to pin him down and I could finally speak to him face-to-face and have all my questions answered…It would be a hard dream to let go of. "Let's see if we can figure out where he is going. If we can pin him down, we'll decide then what to do with that information."

Tony nodded. "Okay. Now that I have a very specific starting place, I can adjustment the program. We should start getting regular hits. Not as many as we would if he was in a big city with traffic cams, but I'm confident we should be able to establish a pattern. If it looks like he is staying put, our next decision will be whether or not to make the trip to connect with him."

He went to the table and logged on to his laptop. He pulled up a map and entered the GPS coordinates of my father's current location. He then logged on to his program and tightened the search parameters. It occurred to me that if we could track him in real time, others with Tony's level of expertise could as well. Not that there were many people in the world with Tony's level of expertise, but there had to be some. I had to wonder if the fact that my dad hadn't really changed his look after faking his death wasn't putting him in danger from whoever he was hiding from.

Tony looked up at me. "I am going to have the program focus on hits in real time. That will mean that the program will no longer be looking for photos from the past, but it seems that now that we know your dad is alive, the most important information to gather is where he might be going rather than where he has been."

"I agree."

"Now that I have an actual GPS location to use as a starting point, the program is going to focus on additional hits from nearby places. This may or may not work. Unfortunately, there aren't a lot of security systems in this part of the country connected to the internet, and as I said before, we don't have the advantage of the traffic cams they have in larger cities."

"I guess we'll just see what we can find. To be honest, I'm not even sure whether I want to pin him down. If we do, I am going to have a very hard decision to make."

Tony offered me a look of compassion. "There really are a whole lot of ways that continuing with our search could come back to bite us. I think that we should proceed with extreme caution."

"Agreed."

Tony logged off his computer. "Our dinner should be ready. I'll set out the food if you want to refill our wineglasses."

"I wonder if my dad has been alone all this time."

Tony took the casserole out of the oven and set it on a hot pad on the counter. "I suppose if he really was concerned about others getting hurt based on proximity to him, he might have avoided relationships. He does seem to get around, however. I don't have the impression of a man sitting alone in some little apartment. If I had to guess, I'd say he is involved in some sort of work that requires travel."

"Like he did when he was a truck driver."

"Exactly. Although it does seem as if he travels internationally and somehow manages to do so under the radar. Sure, he has a new name and identity, but he didn't change his look, which means he is trackable. We've proved that."

I set both wineglasses on the table, along with the remainder of the bottle. "Do you think he works for the government?"

Tony shrugged as he poured his homemade dressing over the salad. "Perhaps. Or he might work for a private firm or individual with connections in high places. His movements have the feel of the CIA or maybe even a black ops group to me, but unless we find something linking him to a specific organization, all we have is conjecture."

I sat down at the table and waited for Tony to join me. There was one question in my mind that I couldn't quite bring myself to voice, yet it was always in the forefront of my mind. Whatever my dad was in to, was he a good guy or a not-so-good one? I hoped that we would find that he worked for the CIA or some other government agency, but for all I knew, he might be a spy working against them.

"I should probably head home after we eat," Tony said. "I can only do so much from my laptop. If we really want to tighten the net, I need to set up some precise parameters I can only do from my supercomputer."

"Okay."

"Do you want to come with me? I can drive you into town in the morning for work."

"I'll come with you, but I'll drive my Jeep. It isn't supposed to snow. I'll take Tang and Tinder and leave them at your place. If I am going to be staying with you full time for a few months, we may as well start the migration."

Tony put his hand over mine and gave it a squeeze. "I know the waiting will be hard."

I smiled and looked Tony in the eye. "It won't be hard. I have you and two other mysteries to focus on."

Tony chuckled. "That's true. I may have a new lead on the missing fiancé."

I took a bite of the spicy Mexican casserole. "What did you find?"

"A man named Michael Patrick O'Malley the Third lived in New Jersey in 1959, but my research indicates that his family lived in Boston. He was twenty-four years old and the eldest son of Michael Patrick O'Malley Junior, who had recently inherited a dry-cleaning empire from his father, Michael Patrick Senior. The second Michael Patrick wasn't interested in dry cleaning, so he sold the business his father built and opened a small neighborhood financial institution he called O'Malley's Savings and Loan. His son, who went by Patrick, was sent to college to obtain the necessary business skills to eventually take over that business. As best as I can tell, Patrick came to White Eagle for the summer after he received his MBA. He was spending the summer with friends and then would be returning to school for a doctorate in finance."

"Sounds like Patrick had big plans for his father's little bank."

"Actually, Michael O'Malley was the one who wanted to grow the institution. Patrick, from what I was able to uncover, seemed to want to study cooking. He wanted to open his own restaurant."

I paused to let this all sink in. "Okay. I guess that fits with what Elizabeth told her granddaughter. She said that she and Patrick planned to run away and start a new life. That fits with the idea that Patrick wasn't thrilled with the life he'd been planning before meeting her. What happened after he left White Eagle to go home?"

"I don't know exactly. Most of what I have learned about Patrick was from a magazine article published years after his death by his sister Gwendolyn, who was a freelance writer. The article was actually about how the death of her brother had affected her and caused her to reevaluate her life. She wrote about a young man who longed for a life different from the one his father had envisioned for him, who never could work up the courage to defy his family and follow his dreams. She mentioned her brother's decision to take some time off from school before entering his doctoral program, and how the trip he took seemed to have changed him. She shared with her readers the fact that he had told her about his intention to go after his own dreams, but that he had died before he'd had the chance to do so. She went on to write about the moment when it struck her that although it was too late for him, it wasn't for her. That was when she decided to drop out of college and become a writer."

"Do we know how he died?"

"Gwendolyn didn't go into specifics about Patrick's death. The article was more about how his death affected her."

"Do you think Gwendolyn is still alive?"

Tony nodded. "She is living in New York and is quite a famous novelist. I think I can track down a way to contact her, but I decided that before I did that, I should speak to you. We should also probably try to confirm that Gwendolyn's Patrick is indeed Elizabeth's Patrick."

"I'll text Jennifer Anne to see if she has a photo of Patrick. I'd like to be sure we have the right man before we tell Elizabeth about his death."

"I'll see if I can't dig a little deeper once we get back to my place. I should also be able to track down an obituary for Patrick now that we have more information. It may include details about his death."

"Okay. Let me pack some stuff to get by for a few days. We can work on moving more of my stuff to your place this weekend."

Chapter 7

Wednesday, March 20

I'd texted Jennifer Anne after we arrived at Tony's place and asked if she had a photo of Patrick. She wasn't sure if Elizabeth had one, but she would ask and let me know. Tony set to work creating a net that he hoped would help us narrow in on my father's current whereabouts. In the event he was staying in Billings and hadn't just been passing through, he hoped to come up with an actual location where we might find and confront him, if that was what I chose to do. Honestly, I wasn't sure what I wanted, and I wasn't sure what, if anything, I should tell Mike. If I knew my brother—and I did—if he thought our father was in Montana, he'd be on the next commuter flight south. In some ways, Mike was as much of a hothead as my dad, and I didn't see a meeting between the two going well.

I was glad I had my route to take my mind off everything else the next day. I settled into a comfortable rhythm as Tilly and I delivered the mail and caught up on the latest news.

"Afternoon, Frank," I said as we stopped by the police station to drop off the day's mail. "Any news on Brick's murder?"

"Not really, although I do have a new theory."

"And what is that?"

"I'm wondering if the original sample isn't from a crime of some sort. The person who committed the crime left behind DNA, but it didn't match anything or anyone in the system. Brick had four suspects in mind, so he collected DNA from all the suspects and had it tested."

"Wouldn't you know about it if a crime had occurred?"

"Probably. But not all crimes are reported, and I'm just brainstorming at this point."

"What sort of crime might not be reported that would leave DNA evidence?" I wondered.

"Rape comes to mind. Not every victim is willing to file a police report. Maybe one of Brick's cocktail waitresses was the victim. Brick is pretty protective of his girls. What if one of them was raped, but she didn't know for certain who had done it? Maybe it was dark, or maybe she was blindfolded so she couldn't see who it was, but she suspected it was one of four men. Maybe Brick gathered evidence from them and had it compared to the DNA evidence left at the scene of the rape. Again, this is just a story I am making up right now, but it demonstrates a scenario that makes sense."

I nodded. "It does make sense. Would that same sort of scenario work for crimes committed in the past?"

Frank shrugged. "Sure, I guess. Why do you ask?"

"I spoke to Sue Wade yesterday. She had her own DNA tested against other Wade family members after Austin admitted that he wasn't a Wade by birth. She was the one who told Brick about Genocom. He asked her if it was possible to test old DNA samples, and she told him she didn't know, though she didn't think DNA had an expiration date. Sue imagined that perhaps Brick had something like an old brush with hair in it that he was trying to use to identify the owner."

"Like maybe he was given the brush and told that it had belonged to someone he had been looking for, like a missing sister or a long-lost mother," Frank said. "Maybe he had narrowed it down to four possibilities but needed confirmation of which of the three was the person he was seeking."

"That works as well," I said. "We are going to need to find additional clues to figure out who Brick might have been trying to identify through the testing." I looked up as Mike walked into the reception area from the hallway. "Any luck getting Genocom to voluntarily give up the names associated with the DNA?"

"No," Mike answered my query, "but I'm still working on trying to get to someone with the authority to make an executive decision and give me the information without a court order."

"I still think the letter with the handwritten address might provide a clue," I said. "It was delivered at around the same time as everything else. Did you ever figure out who turned the open box you found over to Brick?"

Mike shook his head. "No one is fessing up to it. It may not even be important, but given everything else that we are putting together, I sure would like to know what was in the box."

"You said there wasn't a return address, but if there was a tracking number or even a postmark, maybe we can find out where it came from. Do you have the box here?"

"In my office."

"Let's take a look."

Mike walked down the hallway and I followed. He picked up the box and handed it to me as soon as we entered his office.

"Iowa." I frowned. "The letter with the handwritten address originated in Iowa too. I'd be willing to bet they are connected."

"So we have a letter and a report from Genocom, which was delivered on a Tuesday. We have a letter with an Iowa postmark, a handwritten address, but no return address, delivered on a Thursday. We also have a box from Iowa that was delivered to the local post office on Friday for delivery on the following Monday, but Brick somehow obtained possession of it before he died on Saturday."

I nodded. "And the large envelope I thought might contain a magazine or a catalog but can't be sure that it was either. That was delivered on Thursday as well. We need to take another look around Brick's home and office. That handwritten note seems to be the missing link and it has to be somewhere."

"Unless the killer knew about it and took it," Mike pointed out.

"Well, yeah, I guess there's that. By the way, did you ever figure out whose whiskey we found in Brick's office?"

"There were no fingerprints on the glass, and it appeared that while someone poured the drink, they didn't take a single sip."

"Figures. I need to get back to my route, but if you find anything new, you can text me."

I called Tilly and headed out of the station. I still had both Bree's bookstore and my mom's restaurant to deliver to. Both stops were guaranteed to be long ones. Maybe they would be busy and wouldn't have time to chat. I supposed I could always text Tony to let him know that I might be late getting home. Of course, getting home and finding out if he had made progress on our other two mysteries was the very thing I most wanted to do.

"Afternoon, Bree," I said as Tilly and I entered her store.

"Tess, I'm so glad you're here. I am having another wedding emergency and you are just the one to help me figure it out."

"Okay. What's the problem?"

"Mike and I went to talk to the event coordinator at The Lakehouse last night. I really think that we might have found a venue, but I need to put down a deposit by the end of the day if we want her to hold it for us. The problem is, they have noise regulations for all outdoor events that forbid the use of live bands or almost anything other than the most subdued music after ten o'clock."

"I guess that makes sense. There are homes in the area."

"That's what the woman said. But the plan we talked about, with the dinner first, followed by the ceremony and then the dancing, would mean we'd need to have music after ten. The woman said a stereo playing subdued music—the kind you'd find in a fine restaurant—was all right after ten, but a live band or any sort of system with large speakers was out."

I slipped my bag off my shoulder and handed Tilly a treat. I could see this might take more than a few minutes. "Okay, so I see that you have several options. Either find another venue without the music limitation. Or you could move things up so that the entire reception, including the dancing, is over by ten. Or just plan on slow dancing to elevator music."

"Mike really wants to have a live band. I think it was the number one thing on his list. My silly vows-under-the-stars thing is what is messing everything up. If not for that, we could have the ceremony at six, drinks immediately after, dinner at seven, and then dancing from eight to ten. We could do dinner and dancing to end at ten and get married last, but doing the vows after dancing really would seem anticlimactic."

"You could get married in December. It's dark by like four thirty in December."

"And it is also too cold for an outdoor wedding," Bree said.

"What if your wedding and reception were separate events?"

Bree frowned. "What do you mean?"

"Getting married under the stars seems really important to you, but it doesn't work with a big reception with a live band and a catered dinner like Mike wants. What if you exchange your vows on Friday, with just the family? We could do it at Tony's and have dinner after. Then, you can have a huge reception at The Lakehouse with a catered meal and a band on Saturday, if it's available then. You could start at five or six and wrap it up by ten."

Bree narrowed her gaze. "Would that be weird?"

I put my hands on Bree's shoulders. "This is your wedding. Do what you want. The only people whose opinions matter are yours and Mike's. Talk to him. My guess is that he will be all for a smaller group for the actual ceremony."

Bree hugged me. "Okay. I'll call him right now. I think your plan might just work."

Mentally adding another check in the best-maid-of-honor-ever column, Tilly and I went on our way. I figured I'd stop by the restaurant toward the end of my route. If I popped in then, when Mom and Aunt Ruthie were ready to go home, maybe they wouldn't pull me into a long conversation. I crossed the street and headed toward Grandma Hattie's Bakeshop.

"Afternoon, Hattie," I said as I handed her a stack of mail. "Something smells wonderful."

"I've got gingersnaps in the oven. Special order for the Cub Scout meeting this afternoon."

"Lucky kids. I never did have lunch. I don't suppose you have something I can eat while I finish my route?"

"I have fresh blueberry muffins."

"Perfect."

Hattie opened a white to-go bag and slipped a muffin inside while Tilly walked over to say hi to Hattie's dog, Bruiser.

"Any news about Brick's murder?" Hattie asked after handing me the bag. "I know you tend to have an ear to the ground."

"I know that Mike and Frank are looking at several different scenarios."

"I heard that Dover Boswell was a suspect."

I shook my head. "He was interviewed, but Mike told me he had an alibi for the night Brick was killed. I still don't know where the truth lies in terms of him stealing from Brick, but I suppose that isn't the important matter at this point. Did Brick ever say anything to you about DNA testing?"

Hattie shook her head. "Not that I recall. At least not recently. He popped in a few months ago after closing. I was cleaning up and had *Cold Case Files* on in the background. He made a comment about liking the show, and we had a conversation about how new DNA tests that were unavailable years ago were currently being used to solve decades-old cold cases. He seemed interested, so I told him about the guy who killed eight women more than thirty years ago only to be arrested all these years later after he signed up for one of those ancestry accounts and voluntarily submitted his DNA, which provided the feds with a match for the DNA left on one of the victims at the time of the murders. Crazy, isn't it?"

"It is crazy. Did Brick mention having DNA he wanted to test?"

Hattie shook her head. "No. But he did get a look when I told him the story."

"A look?"

"His eyes grew big. It seemed he was interested in what I had to say. I almost felt like my story hit home with him in some way. You don't think that is what got him killed?"

"No, probably not. I was just curious. It seems there are a lot of rumors going around and it is hard to know what is fact and what is fiction."

Hattie let out a short laugh. "Yeah, there are a lot of rumors all right. I even heard that Brick was doing drugs, which is just nonsense. The man was known to drink from time to time, but I'm quite sure he never messed around with anything harder than a whiskey at the end of the day. Folks like to be involved, so they spout off about things they don't know anything about. But doing so risks the reputation of those who aren't here to defend themselves. It just isn't right."

"I totally agree." I glanced at the clock on the wall. "Listen, I need to get going. Thanks for the muffin."

"Any time, my dear. I'll save you a couple of gingersnaps for when you come by tomorrow."

Tilly and I headed out into the sunshine. We needed to pick up the pace. We made good time with our next ten stops before coming to the last one of the day: Sisters' Diner.

"Tess honey, I was wondering what had become of you," Mom greeted me.

"I met with Mike and got behind. I've been playing catch-up all day, but you are my last stop. I can't stay long, though. Tony is expecting me."

"Met with Mike? Are you helping him with the murder case?"

"I wouldn't say helping exactly, but he wanted me to help identify some mail I delivered in the week before Brick was shot. I bet everyone who comes in to eat here has something to say about it."

Aunt Ruthie came out to the seating area from the kitchen. She must have heard us talking. "Everyone does seem to have an opinion about what is going on," she said. "I even heard a couple of men who were in the same bowling league as Brick say that the killer was a hired gun."

I frowned. "I doubt that. Why did they think so?"

Ruthie shrugged. "I really don't know. If you ask me, they were just spouting off about things they knew nothing about, but I did notice that they managed to pull others who were seated in their vicinity into their conversation. I wouldn't be a bit surprised to hear that the hired gun theory has made the rounds of all the local gossip groups by tomorrow."

I handed Mom a stack of mail. "I really should get going. Tony is working on a project with Shaggy, so he is going to be in town for a while. I think the kids and I are going to be staying out at his place as long as the weather holds. I'll have my cell, but I wanted to let you know in case you noticed I wasn't at the cabin."

"And dinner on Sunday?"

I cringed. "I'm sorry; I forgot to ask Tony about it. I'll call you later to confirm, but as far as I know, it should work fine." *Unless I am in Billings, tracking down Dad*, I added in my head.

Chapter 8

I had to admit that I was getting pretty spoiled, having dinner ready for me each evening when I got home from work. Tony enjoyed cooking and he seemed to love having someone to cook for, so I knew I shouldn't feel like I was taking advantage of him, but I did.

"I smell garlic," I said as I walked in through the front door with Tilly on my heels.

Tilly greeted Tony and then trotted over to say hi to Titan.

"It's linguine with broccoli, pine nuts, green olives, and feta cheese, topped with a buttery garlic sauce."

I tossed my backpack onto a nearby chair. "Oh, I love your linguine with garlic sauce. Tonight is a good time to have it because I'm starving. All I managed to find time to eat was a muffin Hattie gave me for the road."

"It's just about ready and I have salad as a starter, so if you want to run up and change, I'll get everything on the table."

I kissed Tony on the lips. "Thank you. You are the king of boyfriends."

Tony chuckled. "I do try. Do you want wine?"

"Maybe a glass with dinner. I'm hoping we have new clues to discuss."

"I've managed to find a few more pieces to the puzzle, but I won't go so far as to say I have any major breakthroughs to discuss. Go and change and we'll talk while we eat."

I jogged up the stairs to the bedroom Tony and I shared. He had a large house, and every room in it was pretty amazing, but I especially loved the effort he had taken to ensure that I would feel comfortable in the previously spartan bedroom. He'd purchased a new bed, as well as new furniture that had a woodsy feel that perfectly accentuated the river-rock fireplace and the wood-framed windows that looked out onto the private lake that occupied the center of his property. He'd convinced me to pick out new bedding in a color I liked, as well as a couple of soft, comfy chairs in which we could read in front of the fire on cold winter nights. During the warmer months, a glass door led out to a private deck that featured an outdoor fireplace, cozy deck furniture, and an outdoor spa in one corner. The bedroom was almost as large as my entire cabin if you added in the attached bath, which had seemed sort of extravagant to me initially, but after enjoying the comfort the room provided, I could see how one could get used to living an extravagant lifestyle.

After changing into jeans and a long-sleeved T-shirt, I headed back downstairs. Tony had set the table in the kitchen nook, which provided a wonderful view of the mountains.

"I have to say, I could easily get used to coming home to this every night."

Tony poured my wine. "That is my evil plan."

"Did you talk to Shaggy about the project?"

Tony sat down across from me. "I did. I think he is about as psyched about it as I've ever seen him, and this is the man who did cartwheels down Main Street when the new Zombie Hunters video game was released."

I laughed. "Shaggy possesses a certain childlike quality that I both admire and find irritating. When are you going to start working on the new game?"

"Right away. He is going to come over on Saturday while you are dog training with Brady. We'll use the time to map out the basic concept. Once I have that, I can start coding a mock-up that we can use to test our ideas. The project as a whole will take a while to complete, but I'm really looking forward to it."

"Before I forget, my mom wants us to come to dinner on Sunday. I'm sure she is going to invite Mike and Bree as well."

"I'd enjoy that. I always like spending time with your family."

"I figured you would be fine with it, but I wasn't sure how our search for my dad might interfere with any plans we might make."

Tony set down his fork. He turned and looked at me. "The tight net I set up and hoped would provide us with additional localized hits didn't result in anything, so I widened the parameters a bit and got a hit today from Saint Paul, Minnesota. It appears your dad is on the move and heading east at a fairly brisk pace. Anticipating his route will help us to focus our search and, I anticipate, will result in additional sightings, but it doesn't seem as if he is going to be staying in one area, as we initially hoped. Again, I have to ask if you want me to continue to track him. If he is working for an agency or an individual with the capabilities we believe he has, he is going to figure out at some point that we are tracking him."

"Let's just keep an eye on his movements for now. I need to think things through. Part of me believes I should let it go and get on with my life, but another part that still wonders about the specifics hates to let go of the lead we have now that we seem to have an idea of where he may be heading."

"If he picks up on the fact that we are tracking him, he may change his travel plans and lose him anyway, but for now, I'll continue down the path I anticipate he is traveling and see where we end up. Have you said anything to Mike?"

I shook my head. "He'd just go off on a rampage and give up everything he is doing here to try to track him down. I'm sort of sorry that we told him what we did. Now that he knows that, I feel like I am lying to him by not keeping him in the loop, but he has a murder to solve and a wedding to plan, and the last thing he needs to be distracted by is a manhunt he is likely to come out on the losing end of."

"I agree that we aren't likely to catch up with your dad unless he wants to be caught up with. I almost wonder if he already knows about the hits we got over the past couple of days and is intentionally letting us know where he is."

"Why would he do that?"

"I have no idea. I've never met him. I just think that he is skilled in the art of staying under the radar. For us to get two pretty plump hits in two days almost makes me think he intentionally let himself be photographed."

Well, wouldn't that be a twist. Could my dad actually be communicating with us or, more likely, playing with us?

"Was there anything unusual about the video images that matched up?" I asked.

"What do you mean by unusual?"

"Your program picked up images captured by surveillance cameras, right?"

"The image captured in Billings was from a surveillance camera and the one in Saint Paul from a traffic cam. He ran a red light."

"Don't you think that it is odd for a man in hiding to run a red light in an area patrolled by traffic cams?"

"You think he intentionally ran the red light? Why?"

"Maybe he knows we are tracking him and he is playing with us."

Tony frowned. "Seems risky. If your dad is on the run from someone, I would think he would have to assume that the someone he is hiding out from has access to the same facial recognition software I have. In fact, if he is on the run from a government agency, you can bet their software is even better than mine."

I poked at my linguine. "Getting caught on a traffic cam seems sloppy and careless. My dad was neither."

"Maybe someone was following him and stopping for a red light was not an option."

I supposed Tony had a point. If my dad was being pursued, maybe running the light was the least objectionable move available to him. I picked up my fork and started eating again. "So, any new developments in the case of the missing fiancé?"

"I have contact information for Patrick's sister Gwendolyn. I wasn't sure what you wanted to do about it, so I haven't done anything yet."

"We should confirm that we have the right Patrick before I pass the information on to Jennifer Anne. Did you find the obituary? Do we know how Patrick died?"

"I haven't found an obituary or any other information about Patrick's death."

"Let's contact Gwendolyn and explain the situation. We'll decide how to proceed after we get a feel for her reaction."

Tony took a sip of his wine. "All right. Do you want another piece of bread?"

"No, I'm good. The food was delicious. I'll help you with the dishes and then we can relax. I'd love to take the dogs for a walk. The sun has set, but the snow has melted and the lake trail is pretty dry. I think we'll do fine with flashlights."

"Sounds good to me. I could use a walk. I wanted to talk to you about Italy. We can talk while we walk."

"Italy?"

"I'd like us to go to visit my nona. I know that you are busy with the wedding now, but maybe in the fall. If we can find someone to watch the animals, that is."

Italy in the fall. That sounded magical.

"Run and grab us jackets," Tony said. "I'll put the leftovers away before we go. I can wash the dishes when we get back."

By the time I returned with the jackets, the food was stored and the dogs were ready to go out.

"I remember you said your nona lived in a small village in Northern Italy," I said as we walked. "Are there hotels in her village?"

"No, but Nona would never allow us to stay in a hotel anyway. She has a guest room."

"And she won't mind us staying in the guest room together?"

Tony laughed. "Not at all. As long as she approves of you as the bearer of her great-grandchildren, she'll be pushing us together."

I coughed. "Great-grandchildren? We are just going for a visit?"

Tony squeezed my hand. "We are just going for a visit, but Nona is the sort to make a judgment about people upon first meeting them."

"That sounds intimidating."

"Don't worry; she is going to love you. How could she not?"

"Have you brought other girls to meet her?" I found myself asking.

"Never, which is why Nona will realize right away that you are special. I don't want you to worry about her liking you. I promise, she will love you just as I do. She is, after all, an excellent judge of character."

Suddenly, a romantic trip to Italy felt more like an interview for the job of Tony's wife and the mother of Nona's great-grandchildren. I wasn't sure how I felt about that.

"I'll have to see if I can get time off work." I found myself backing away from the idea.

"We have months to work out the details. I just wanted to open a dialogue. I know you will love Italy. The scenery, the food, the simple yet traditional way of life. And if you want to extend our trip, we could visit Rome as well. I want to show you the world of my roots."

"It does sound wonderful. Let's get through Mike and Bree's wedding and then talk about it again. I'm not sure I can take on another source of stress right now."

The sky was beginning to darken, so Tony clicked on his flashlight. "Have they worked out the details for the wedding?"

"I'm not sure. I did suggest having the ceremony itself here under the stars followed by a dinner made by you on Friday if they wanted to focus on the reception on Saturday. I don't know if that is what they will decide to do. I suppose I should have asked you first."

"There was no need to ask. I am always happy to do what I can for any member of your family. They don't want to be married on the same day as the reception?"

I explained the very real problems created by trying to give Bree her fantasy of being married under the stars in June.

"That's probably going to be a problem anywhere given the fact that it gets dark so late during the summer. If Mike and Bree decide to have the ceremony here at the lake, I will make them a feast fit for royalty. How many people do you think they'll want to invite?"

"I know they will want the family to be there, which would include Mom, Aunt Ruthie, Ruthie's son Johnnie and his family, Ruthie's daughter Lisa and her family, Bree's mom and sister, and the two of us. Frank is going to be Mike's best man, so he'll be there too. Beyond that, I'm not sure."

"We'll make a Friday ceremony special if that's what they choose to do. But if they decide to forget about the solstice and do it all on Saturday, that will be special as well. Every bride should have her perfect day."

"It looks like there is a car in your drive," I said as we rounded the last corner that led back to the house.

"I see."

"I don't recognize it. Do you?"

"No." Tony glanced at the car and frowned. "Head in the back door with the dogs. I'll go see who it is and what they want."

I called the dogs to follow me. Titan especially clearly wanted to follow Tony, but he told him to stay with me and he obeyed. The dogs and I slipped through the kitchen door, and then I headed toward the front of the house. I hoped I would be able to hear what was being said through the door, but no one was talking loud enough, and they hadn't approached the house from the driveway. After a few minutes, I saw two men get back into the car and drive off, and Tony returned to the house.

"Who was it?" I asked. "What did they want?"

"They said they were with the CIA. They had ID, but I had an odd feeling about their authenticity."

"You think the ID was fake?"

"Maybe."

"What'd they want?"

"They know we have been looking for your dad and they asked if we had a lead on his whereabouts."

"What did you tell them?"

"That we had stopped looking and didn't know where he was. They said they had intel that he was in Montana as recently as a few days ago and asked if he tried to contact you. I told them he hadn't."

"So if the men are from the CIA and they're looking for my dad, that must mean that isn't who he's working for."

"It would seem not if they are, in fact, CIA, which, as I've said, I am less than sure about."

"If they are CIA, do you think the CIA is watching us watching Dad?"

"I think that would be exactly what they are doing."

"Which is another reason to stop looking. We still don't know why my dad faked his death or even whether he is a good guy or a bad guy, but I do know that if those men are after him, I don't want to be the one to lead them to him. Turn off your tracking program. I knew after our trip to the lake that it might be time to let Dad fade away, as he clearly wants to do. This convinces me even more that letting go of my search for my dad is the right thing to do."

Chapter 9

Friday, March 22

It had been two days since I'd made the decision to stop tracking my dad, and in that time, I'd questioned myself at least a hundred times. I knew it was probably the best thing to do if our tracking Dad might lead someone else to him, but not having had the opportunity to confront him to ask the questions that had been churning in my gut for all these years left me feeling unsatisfied. I knew that the smartest thing I could do was to focus on something else, so I checked in with Mike to see if he had any updates on the murder case.

"Good morning, Tess, Tilly. You're here early today," Frank greeted us.

"I changed things up today." I slipped my mailbag off my shoulder as Tilly went over to greet Leonard, who'd come running down the hall when he heard us come in. "Any news about Brick Brannigan's murder?"

"I'm not sure what Mike has already told you, so you might want to check with him. He's in his office."

"I'm right here," Mike said, stepping into the room from the hallway.

"It's been a couple of days since we chatted, and I was curious if you ever found either the handwritten letter or the contents of the second large envelope. Or the contents of the box you found, for that matter."

"So far, we've had no luck with any of those things. Without knowing what was in the box or the second large envelope, it is hard to know if we've come across the items contained within and just aren't aware of it. As for the letter with the handwritten address, we've looked for it, but so far, no go."

"I wonder what Brick did with the letter if you've searched the bar and his home," I said.

"Maybe Brick tossed or burned it," Frank suggested.

"It didn't look as if he tossed or destroyed a single piece of correspondence he received since he bought the bar," I responded. "There were envelopes, junk mail, and old letters everywhere."

"Maybe the envelope you are looking for contained damning information and Brick destroyed it to keep anyone from reading it."

"Maybe," I acknowledged.

"What about the postmark being from Iowa?" Frank asked.

"Useless," Mike said. "At least without more information."

I nodded. "We can use the postmark to backtrack to the city of origin, but unless someone from the post office remembers who posted the box, which I highly doubt, I agree the postmark is useless. Has anyone looked inside the pockets of Brick's jacket? I assume it was hanging in the bar?"

"His pockets were empty," Mike confirmed.

"What about his truck? Has anyone looked between the seats, in the glove box, or on the floor?"

Mike glanced at Frank. "You searched the truck."

"I was looking for a smoking gun, not a letter."

"We should take another look," I said.

"I'll do it," Frank offered.

"What about the identity of the four samples that Brick had tested? Did you ever get anyone from Genocom to provide you with names to go with the letters on the reports?"

Mike nodded. "Yes and no. I did finally make my way far enough up the hierarchy to speak to someone with the authority to give me the information I need. I even got this person to agree to provide me with what I requested."

"And?" I asked.

"And names were never provided. Brick sent in four samples: L, B, S, and A. That was the way he labeled them. He asked them to provide as much information as possible for each sample, and it seems he paid them a boatload of money for it."

"And they did it without names or permission from those involved?"

"Apparently."

"It sounds like maybe our theory fits that Brick had possession of someone's DNA but no one to compare it to. Still, I'm not sure how we are supposed to match the DNA with actual people."

"I agree that we aren't going to figure this out without more information," Mike said.

"My gut tells me that Brick had DNA from a crime scene. All the secrecy doesn't make a lot of sense if he was simply looking for a long-lost relative. Maybe we can go back and look at unsolved crimes in the area over the past five years or so," I suggested.

"The DNA sample would give us the hair and eye color if we knew how to read the darn thing," Frank said. "We should be able to figure out sex and nationality as well."

"The report was thirty pages long. I bet there is additional information beyond that that will help us create a visual of the individuals," I said. "What we need is a forensic scientist. Maybe there is someone at the crime lab who can help you, or someone from the lab can refer you to a specialist in this area."

"I'll check," Mike said.

I glanced at Frank. "I need to start my route. Call my cell if you find the letter in the truck. I'll see if Tony has time to help you track down cold cases. I have a feeling that one of those cases is going to connect with subject K."

My next stop was Grandma Hattie's Bakeshop, where I was gifted with a bag of hot-from-the-oven oatmeal cookies. By the time I made it to Hap's store, I was buzzing right along. It wasn't until I left Cartwright's Furniture that I took a minute to check my phone messages. There was one from Tony, asking me to call him.

"Hey, what's up?" I asked when he picked up.

"I spoke to Gwendolyn O'Malley. I told her the story of Elizabeth and Patrick, and she said she would like to meet Elizabeth and Jennifer Anne."

"I thought she lived in New York."

"She does. But she is in Seattle as part of a book tour and could arrange to spend time with them if I am able to get them there. My buddy with the jet can take us to Seattle tomorrow if we want, but I wasn't sure how you wanted me to proceed."

I paused to consider the situation. I supposed if we had the right Patrick, Gwendolyn was Jennifer Anne's great-aunt. It made sense that she might want to have the opportunity to speak with a woman claiming to have born her dead brother's child face-to-face. "I'm sure I can get someone to cover for me with the dog training session tomorrow. I'll call Jennifer Anne to see what she wants to do. I'll call you back as soon as I speak to her."

I decided to continue my route and wait to make the call until I got to Sisters' Diner, where I could grab a cup of coffee while I took my break. I called the cell number Jennifer Anne had given me, and luckily, she picked up right away. I shared the news about the article written by the woman we believed to be Patrick's sister, as well as her desire to meet Jennifer Anne and her grandmother. She wasn't certain how Elizabeth would react, so she told me she would speak to her and call me back within the hour.

"I spoke to Mike earlier," my mom said, sliding into the booth across from me. "He said that you had suggested to Bree that she might want to have the wedding ceremony the day before the reception."

I picked up the coffee cup Mom had brought me and took a sip. "Bree is still struggling with the whole vows-under-the-stars thing. I just don't see how they can do that and have the big catered reception with a live band that Mike wants. By having a family-only ceremony on Friday and the reception with all their friends on Saturday, they can both get what they want."

"I will admit that when Mike first shared the idea, I wasn't a fan of dividing the two parts, but the more I think about it, the more sense it makes. We can talk about it some more on Sunday when you all come for dinner. I'm planning to do a pot roast, which is Mike's favorite, so he should be in an amiable mood."

"I'm looking forward to it. There is a possibility I may be out of town tomorrow." I explained about the missing fiancé Tony and I were helping to track down.

"You are going to fly to Seattle for the day?" Mom asked.

"That's the plan, if Jennifer Anne's grandmother agrees to it," I said.

"On a private jet?"

I nodded. "The jet belongs to a friend of Tony's. I won't know for sure if we are making the trip until I hear back from the granddaughter, but I wanted to let you know that I could be out of town if it all comes together."

"I can't imagine someone you love simply disappearing from your life without an explanation. It must be the worst kind of torture."

I thought about my dad, and the fact that he had basically done that exact thing, although as far as Mom knew, he had died rather than disappeared. "I'm sure that Elizabeth has had to deal with all sorts of emotions relating to the uncertainty of it all." I stood up and slipped on my mailbag. Tilly slid out from under the table. "Thanks for the coffee. I really need to get going if I want to stay on time today. I'll text you tomorrow if we do end up going to Seattle."

After I left my mom's restaurant, I continued on down the block. I'd already dropped off the mail at the police station when I was there that morning, but I decided to pop in to see if Frank had found the letter we'd been looking for as long as I was in the vicinity.

"Hey, Frank. I was passing by and wanted to see if you found the letter that went with the handwritten address."

"I didn't, but I did find something interesting in the cargo area of Brick's truck. It didn't stand out as relevant when I looked through the truck in the first place, but now that we know about the DNA testing, it jumped right out at me."

"And what was that?"

"Empty vials. They were in a tackle box with some lures and hooks, so I assumed they were meant to take samples of water, although I have no idea why Brick would be sampling water. Now I have to wonder if they were for collecting DNA."

"Why would Brick keep vials in a tackle box?" I asked.

"It seems as good a place as any. A tackle box would keep the glass vials from breaking and it's easy to carry. Plus, everyone knows that Brick liked to fish, so no one would question his having the box with him."

I frowned. "Somehow, the idea that Brick was carrying around vials to use for DNA samples doesn't seem right. Still, I guess he would need a way of sending whatever samples he did collect to Genocom without destroying them. I wonder exactly what he sent. Saliva? Cigarette butts? Maybe chewing gum that had been recently abandoned? This whole thing is so odd." I crossed my arms over my chest. "Do you know if Mike was able to find someone to read the reports Genocom sent?"

"He spoke to someone on the phone. I think he plans to scan the reports into a file and email them to whoever he spoke to. Maybe we'll find a clue once someone who knows what they are looking at takes a peek."

"I hope so." I picked up my bag. "I need to run. Text me if you find anything new. The longer this case goes unresolved, the more curious I become."

"Yeah, it's a complicated one, that's for sure."

Tilly and I continued down the street toward the Book Boutique. From what my mother had said, it sounded as if Mike and Bree had been discussing the wedding. Maybe they'd come to a decision. It would be nice to have the details of time and place decided once and for all. Looking back, I'd thought the biggest issues were going to be the food selection and the band they'd hire, but I guess I should have known there would be challenges every step of the way.

"Hey, Bree," I greeted my best friend.

"Oh good, I hoped you'd be by early today."

Tilly trotted over to say hi to Bree while I took off my bag. "What's up?"

"Mike and I talked about everything, and he is very much in favor of the idea of a smaller ceremony with just the family and then a large reception with all our friends the following evening. I called The Lakehouse and they do have an opening on Saturday, so it is an option. When I told Mike, he said that not only would it solve our conflict between the band and the ceremony under the stars I want, but he feels that having the ceremony over with would allow him to relax and enjoy the reception."

Uh-oh. Having the ceremony over with? Bree didn't look mad, but it seemed like the sort of comment that would make her mad. She seemed happy and was smiling, though, so I let it pass. "That's great. So, do you want to have the ceremony at Tony's by the lake, weather permitting?"

"If it is okay with him."

"I asked him, in the event that was what you decided to do, and he was fine with it. He said he'd cook us all a gourmet meal after. He'll just need a head count and any menu requests you have."

"I'll get both to you in plenty of time. I'm thinking just wedding party and family members. At first, I wasn't sure about the idea, but Mike seemed really relieved. I know he hates to speak in front of crowds, and we plan to write our own vows. I think he will be able to relax and enjoy both the ceremony and the reception if we do it this way." Bree leaned forward and hugged me. "Thank you so much for helping us figure it out."

I smiled. "Happy to help. Did you go ahead and reserve The Lakehouse for the reception?"

"Mike is going to stop by there today to put down a deposit. Now that we have that figured out, we can start planning the other details. Mike wants to do BBQ for the reception. At first, I wasn't so sure that would be right, but I could see that the food and band were the most important things to him, so we divided up the tasks. He is going to decide on the music and the food and I am going to take care of the flowers and décor. He doesn't care about the color scheme, so he said I could pick that as well."

"I'm so glad you worked it out." My cell pinged. "I need to get this."

Bree nodded. "Of course. Go ahead."

"Hey, Jennifer Anne," I said. "Did you speak to your grandmother?"

"I did, and she would like to speak to Gwendolyn. If she really does turn out to be her Patrick's sister, she said she very much wants to meet her. Are you sure you have the transportation worked out?"

"Tony has a friend with a jet. I'll tell him to make the arrangements. I'll call you back in a while with the time and everything else. It will be a very long day. I hope that Elizabeth is up for it."

"She seems determined to get her answers after all this time, so I think she is willing to do whatever needs to be done. She can sleep on the plane if the trip tires her."

"Okay, wonderful. Tony will make the arrangements."

Chapter 10

Saturday, March 23

The flight from Missoula to Seattle was a fairly easy one. Tony had rented a car and arranged to meet Gwendolyn at her hotel at around one. I could see that both Jennifer Anne and Elizabeth were nervous. I guess I didn't blame them. If Gwendolyn was really the sister of Elizabeth's Patrick, the meeting would be an important one for everyone involved.

"You said that Gwendolyn is a writer," Jennifer Anne said as we made the drive from the airport to the hotel. "Do you know what she writes?"

"Women's fiction," Tony responded. "I didn't have time to read any of her work, but I did look her up. She is fairly well known."

"I'm impressed that she took time out of her busy schedule to speak to us."

I smiled at Jennifer Anne. "If it does turn out that you are her grand-niece, I imagine this meeting is as important to her as it is to you."

"And if Nana's Patrick is a different Patrick altogether?"

"Then at least you will know. Tony did ask Gwendolyn if Patrick had been in Montana before he died and she said he was, so my guess is that the man who fathered your mother was indeed Gwendolyn's brother."

"Did she say how Patrick died?" Jennifer Anne asked.

I noticed that got Elizabeth's attention. To this point, Jennifer Anne hadn't asked, and I hadn't volunteered the information, but I supposed it was better to get it out of the way now rather than later. "He went to the bank to take out some cash for his trip back to Montana. He was mugged."

"Oh God." I could see the shock in Jennifer Anne's expression. "I didn't realize he'd been murdered."

I glanced at Elizabeth. A stream of tears ran down her face.

"Gwendolyn told me that after Patrick came home, he met with their father and told him of his plans to move out west to be with his one true love. The two argued, and in the end, their father cut him off. Patrick wasn't going to be swayed, so he sold his car as well as his other belongings and deposited the checks. When he was ready to make the trip back to Montana, he went to the bank to take out the cash and was jumped shortly after leaving it. He might have resisted. No one knows for sure. All that is sure is that his body was found in an alley, he had fatal stab wounds to his chest, his wallet was missing, and the bank receipt from his withdrawal was in his pocket."

"Did the family know about Nana?" Jennifer Anne asked.

"I don't know," I answered. I looked at Tony. He shook his head and informed us that Gwendolyn hadn't said one way or the other.

By the time we arrived at the hotel, we had settled into silence. When I saw how white Elizabeth's face had become, I began to question whether this trip to Seattle had been a good idea. Whether it was or not, we were committed, so I plastered a smile on my face and took Elizabeth by the arm. Jennifer Anne took her other arm and the three of us followed Tony, who walked ahead to open doors, inside.

"Gwendolyn?" I asked a well-dressed woman who was waiting in the reception area for us.

When the woman looked up and her mouth dropped open, I knew.

"You look just like him." Gwendolyn stood up. She wrapped her arms around Jennifer Anne.

Jennifer Anne looked shocked at first; then she released her hold on her grandmother and hugged the woman back.

Gwendolyn took a step back. She placed a hand on Jennifer Anne's cheek. "You have his eyes. And his smile."

Jennifer Anne turned toward her grandmother. "Nana has been telling me that since I was a little girl."

Gwendolyn turned to Elizabeth. "You must be the woman who won Patrick's heart."

"Nana has had a stroke and cannot speak well," Jennifer Anne said.

"Of course," Gwendolyn said. She took Elizabeth by the arm. "Let's have a chat, however we manage to get that accomplished."

Tony and I sat back as Gwendolyn, Jennifer Anne, and Elizabeth got to know one another. Patrick never had told his sister the name of the woman he had fallen in love with, or any way to help identify her. All he'd told her was that he'd met the other half of his heart and planned to build a life with her, following the dreams they had developed together rather than the plans that had been handed to him. He'd been sorry about the rift in his relationship with his father, but in the end, he'd realized that a clean break was the only way.

Gwendolyn had always wondered about the woman Patrick had planned to marry. All she knew was that he'd planned to return to Montana, but Montana was a big place, and without more information, she had no way of contacting Patrick's one true love about his death. He hadn't mentioned the pregnancy, but Elizabeth assured Gwendolyn that he hadn't known about it.

By the time they had to head back to the airport, Gwendolyn had arranged to come to Montana for a long visit with her newly found great-niece once her book tour was over. It was a teary but happy farewell before we got back into the rental car.

"Thank you so very much," Jennifer Anne said to Tony and me as we flew home. Elizabeth was sound asleep. "I can't tell you how much this means to both Nana and me. To think that I've had this other family out there all this time."

"Other than Gwendolyn, are there other relatives you hope to get to know?" I asked.

"Gwen has children and grandchildren. She assured me that they will all be thrilled to meet me. Patrick's parents are dead, but he had another sibling in addition to Gwen, a younger brother who is still alive. Gwen is going to arrange a family reunion of some sort in the near future." Jennifer Anne glanced fondly at her grandmother. "I know this has been a lot for her to take in, but I think that she has found solace in her grief over losing Patrick now that she knows he meant to return to her and has met his sister."

"Do you think that your annual trips to the bench in the park on Saint Patrick's Day will come to an end?"

"Probably not," Jennifer Anne answered. "Nana gave up on the idea that Patrick would show up a very long time ago. I think the trips were more of a way to remember what they'd shared. If I have to guess, as long as she has breath, she will make the trip."

I had a feeling Jennifer Anne was right. Not all the mysteries Tony and I tackled had a happy ending, but it felt to me as if this one had ended about as well as it could have.

Chapter 11

Monday, March 25

Monday started off with a bang when Mike stumbled over a clue in the murder investigation that seemed to put a whole new spin on things.

"Let me get this straight," I said. "The sample from subject K was a clump of hair with follicles intact that have been linked to the murder of a teenage girl that occurred more than twenty years ago?"

"Yes. I'm not sure how Brick got the information required to access the evidence found in the cold case, but the DNA profile for subject K was provided by him, and he then asked the lab to compare the other four samples to the profile provided."

"I'm going to go out on a limb and say that Brick knew the murdered girl."

"It was his sister. Darlene Brannigan was murdered in 1997. She was just sixteen at the time.

The medical examiner found a clump of hair clutched in her hand. It was not hers and was assumed to have belonged to the killer, but a match was never found. The police in Iowa, where she lived, initiated a massive manhunt, but none of the leads they picked up panned out, and eventually, the case went cold. Obviously, Brick never gave up his search for his sister's killer. Given the fact that there were four DNA samples that he wanted tested against the original, he must have narrowed it down to four suspects. It looks as if whoever provided sample L was the killer."

"So how do we figure out who the samples belonged to?" I asked Mike.

"I have no idea, but if I were to guess, figuring out the answer to that question will provide us with the answer not only to who killed Darlene Brannigan but who killed Brick."

"Do either of the other samples match DNA in the law enforcement database?"

"I'm working on it," Mike answered. "Even if the individuals who provided the other samples aren't the person Brick was looking for, knowing that they were suspects could provide us with a clue as to who the fourth individual tested might have been."

"Yeah, I get that. Maybe all four were friends, or they all attended the same party, or they all lived in the town where the murder occurred. I need to get going on my route, but if you need help, or if you come up with new clues, call me right away. Tony is at home working on a video game he is creating with Shaggy, but I'm sure he'd be willing to help out as well. He may not answer the house phone if he is down in the clean room, but you can always email him or send him a message."

"When you get back to the post office at the end of the day, maybe you could ask around about the box Brick somehow took possession of even though it wasn't officially delivered. I'm not sure it is even important at this point, but the box was postmarked from Iowa, which is where Brick's sister was murdered, and that was also the state from which the hand-addressed letter we can't find was sent. I figure whatever was in the box could provide a clue, and someone must know something despite the fact that no one will admit to giving it to him."

"I'll ask around. I'm sure whoever gave the box to Brick just doesn't want to get in trouble for not following protocol."

I thought about the fact that Brick's sister had been murdered as I went about my route. I'd known the guy for a lot of years, but nothing that he had ever said had led me to believe he'd been living with something so horrible in his past. I supposed that murdered sisters weren't something that would come up in everyday conversation, and our relationship had been more of a casual one than a close friendship. But still…

I thought about the locals Brick had been close with. People he might have confided in. Brick seemed to know a lot of people, and there was a whole group who hung out at the bar on a regular basis, but I couldn't think of anyone I would say was a close-enough friend he might have confided in. Brick did have a full-time bartender named Rodney, who I supposed he might have told things to. They spent one-on-one time together while they cleaned up after closing or setting up before opening. I supposed Rodney would be as good a person as any to start with. The bar had been closed since the murder, but I knew that Rodney could be found almost every weekday afternoon at the bowling alley, where he worked as a lane mechanic. The bowling alley wasn't on my route, but I figured if I made good time, I could stop by during my lunch hour, which would need to be a half hour today with all the distractions I'd already had.

"Okay, Tilly, we need to make up some time, so we are in and out. No stopping to chat."

Tilly barked her agreement. I put my head down, grabbed the next stack of mail, and headed into Pete's Pets with a drop-and-run on my mind.

"Hey, Tess, Tilly," Pete said.

"Morning, Pete. I'm in a rush today, so I can't stop to chat. Have a good rest of your day."

"Thanks; you too."

"One down and a whole block to go," I mumbled as I headed into Cartwright's Furniture. Fortunately, Mrs. Cartwright was on the phone when I came in, which allowed me to zip in and out with no more than a friendly smile. The flower shop never really took long because the owner wasn't much of a talker, and there was a line at the ice cream store, thanks to the good weather. I was zipping right along, making up time, when I came to Hap's place. I always stopped to chat with him and couldn't quite bring myself to execute the drop-and-run there, so I plastered on a smile and prepared for a very brief conversation.

"Morning, Hap."

"Tess, Tilly. I hoped I'd be free when you came in. Any news about Brick's murder?"

"Mike is working on it." I placed his mail on the counter. "I know that you chatted with Brick from time to time. I wonder if you knew of anyone he was particularly close to? Anyone he might share stories about his past with, or confide in about his actions in the present?"

"Someone who might know if he had something going on in his life that would have gotten him killed?"

"Exactly."

"Do you know Luke Warner from Warner Construction?"

I nodded. "I know who he is. I can't say I know him well."

"Luke and Brick went fishing sometimes, and Luke hung out at the bar pretty often. I can't say for sure that they shared secrets, but both of them were single, and it seems to me that they hung out about as often as I saw Brick with anyone else."

I thought about Luke. I knew he'd moved to White Eagle a few years back. Initially, he'd worked for a longtime local who had been putting up buildings in the area for decades, but eventually, he set out on his own, and it seemed he was doing pretty well. "Do you happen to know how Brick and Luke knew each other?" I supposed they could have just met at the bar, but it didn't hurt to ask if there was a more specific connection.

"Brick told me he knew him from Iowa."

"Iowa?"

"That's where Brick was originally from. He mentioned being raised on a farm in some little town I don't remember the name of. When he was a teenager, his parents divorced, and he divided his time between his father's farm in Iowa and his mother's place here in Montana."

"So Brick knew Luke when they were kids?"

Hap nodded. "From what I remember Brick telling me."

"Do you know how Brick ended up here in White Eagle?"

Hap shook his head. "Not exactly. Brick mentioned that his mother moved to Missoula after the divorce, so I imagine he might have visited here during that time. I also seem to remember that he lived in Spokane for a while. Spokane isn't all that far away. He might have come to White Eagle to fish or ski. It seems to me that he moved here about fifteen years ago. I don't know if there was a compelling reason for him to do so, or if he just liked the place."

"Did Brick ever talk about his family, other than that his parents were divorced?"

Hap shook his head. "Not really. I guess he had a sister, but he said she died when she was a teenager. It seemed to be a sensitive subject with him, so I didn't pry."

"Thanks, Hap. I'm not sure if Mike is on to something or not, but every little piece of information we are able to dig up seems to help put things together."

"Guess that's the way it works. You just keep collecting pieces until you have an answer to the whole puzzle."

By the time I finished the east side of Main it was lunch time, so I returned to my Jeep and drove to the bowling alley, where I hoped to find Rodney. If he didn't have the answers I was looking for, I'd try to track down Luke after I'd completed my route for the day.

The bowling alley was small, with just eight lanes. When I didn't see Rodney right away, I assumed he wasn't there, but I'd come all this way, so I figured I'd ask. "Rodney around?"

"In the break room."

"I need to talk to him. Is it okay if I go back?"

The man shrugged. "Sure. Whatever."

I thanked him and headed down the short hallway to the room where the employees took their breaks and the lockers for the serious bowlers were kept.

"Hey, Rodney."

"Tess. What are you doing here?"

"I was in the area and decided to stop in to see how you were doing. I know you and Brick were tight."

"*Were* being the operative word."

I wasn't sure what to say.

Rodney went on, saving me the effort of having to come up with a way to phrase my next question. "I guess you heard that Brick fired Dover."

"Yes, I had heard."

"Brick said he stole from him, but I know he didn't. I have no idea what had gotten into Brick, but I do know that at the end, he seemed to have totally lost it."

"Lost it how?"

"The guy was totally paranoid. He thought Dover stole something from him, even though Dover swore he hadn't, and he was sure someone was stalking him."

"Stalking him? Did you tell Mike or Frank this?"

"No. Why should I?"

"Given the fact that he was shot, I would say that he might have been on to something."

Rodney shrugged. "I guess you might have a point."

"Did you work the night Brick was shot?"

"No. I quit my job two days before."

"Why?"

He rolled his eyes. "I just told you, the guy was losing it. I have my job here, and I am usually able to pick up some hours in the bar over on Second Street. I figured I didn't need to put up with Brick's craziness if I didn't want to, and I didn't."

I took a deep breath and let it out slowly. "Did Brick ever say who he thought was stalking him?"

"Not by name. But he did mention something about someone from his past whose comings and goings he had been researching for some reason. I figured that Brick was being stalked, if he really was being stalked, because he himself was a stalker at some point. Look, I'm sorry he is dead. I really am. But it has nothing to do with me, and I'd really like to be left out of things. Now, if you don't mind, the pins in lane two keep getting stuck."

I felt like the information Rodney had tried very hard not to supply was relevant. If Brick thought he had a stalker, he most likely did. The idea that one of the men he was researching had turned it around and begun stalking him seemed like a pretty good theory. I needed to talk to Mike. Maybe this would make sense to him.

Luckily, I found him in his office when I arrived. I filled him in on everything that both Hap and Rodney had told me.

"I spoke to Luke after I found out about Brick's sister," Mike informed me.

"You did? Did you know he was from Iowa?"

Mike nodded. "I pulled the police report from the sister's murder. It seems someone named Luke Warner was one of the people who was interviewed when Darlene's body was found. I knew that Luke and Brick had been friends, and I seemed to remember Brick telling me that he'd known Luke for a long time, so I took a shot that our Luke Warner and the Luke Warner who had been interviewed at the time of Darlene's murder were one and the same. Spoiler alert: they were."

"Was Luke a suspect in Darlene's murder?"

"More like a potential witness. It seems that Luke, who had been good friends with Brick since they were in elementary school, had been casually dating Darlene when she died."

Okay. The plot thickens. "And?"

"And, according to Luke, Darlene had gone to a concert with some friends, so the two of them were not together on the night she died. The investigator was able to verify Luke's alibi and he was not considered a suspect."

I slid off my mailbag, glanced at Tilly, who was playing with Leonard, then settled a hip against Mike's desk. This was going to kill my schedule, but there was no way I was leaving without hearing the rest of the story. "Go on," I encouraged. "What do we know about that night?"

Mike cleared his throat and then continued. "Darlene had gone to a concert with her two best friends, Lacy Tilton and Ginny Lane. The concert featured a heavy metal band whose lyrics and theatrical presentation were geared toward mature audiences, so admittance was limited to those eighteen and over. The three sixteen-year-olds were able to purchase fake IDs that allowed them to attend. Lacy and Ginny were both interviewed after Darlene's murder. They told the police that they had all been drinking and Darlene had begun to feel sick. She excused herself to go find a bathroom. She was never seen alive again by either friend. Her body was found the following morning in an empty field not far away from where the concert was held. Initially, it was assumed that some random person from the concert had killed her and then dumped the body, but Lacy said when interviewed that Darlene had seemed secretive that night, and she wouldn't be at all surprised to find out that Darlene had not been sick, as she'd claimed, but had used the excuse to sneak off to meet someone."

"Why would Darlene lie to her best friends?"

Mike shrugged. "Lacy told the police that it had been Darlene's idea to attend the concert in the first place, and that she had been quite determined to do so. She was the one who obtained the fake IDs and paid for all three tickets."

I paused to let that sink in. "Okay, so Darlene, a minor, seemed to go to a lot of trouble to go to this concert. If the real purpose was to meet up with someone, we should assume this was with someone she wouldn't have just met somewhere else. She told her friends she was feeling sick, then ended up dead. Maybe the person she was meeting killed her, or maybe she ran into someone else while on her way to meet the person she was there to see. I'm not sure we can ever know what she was thinking, but if Brick had four DNA samples and one of them did turn out to be a match for the clump of hair in his sister's hand at the time of her death, we can assume that he figured out who the four most likely suspects were."

"Agreed. Now all we need to do is make the same connection he did."

"Yeah, but he knew the players and we don't. Plus, it was so long ago. Unless your search turns up a match for the DNA samples, I think this is going to be a tough one."

Mike leaned forward and rested his arms on his desk. "I don't disagree, but Brick seemed to have done all the legwork. All we really need to do is figure out what he uncovered. I still think we may be able to find notes or some sort of a clue to lead us to the men he had tested."

I glanced at the clock. "I hope so. I need to get going. I'll talk to you later."

Outside the police station, I glanced up at the sky. "Time to shift into overdrive," I said to Tilly as I picked up the pace and moved down the street.

Chapter 12

"I don't think that Mike told me everything he knows," I said to Tony later that evening as I sat on a barstool in his kitchen and watched him stir-fry onions and peppers into some sort of sauce that smelled heavenly.

"Why do you say that?"

I picked up a piece of the fresh bread Tony had baked, plucked off a corner, and popped it into my mouth. "He opened the conversation by letting me know he had spoken to Luke Warner. Actually, I was the one who'd brought up Luke and suggested that Mike speak to him, which is when he informed me that he had. Anyway, once he told me he had spoken to Luke, the conversation veered onto the subject of how Luke knew Brick and why he was interviewed at the time of Darlene's murder, but he never told me what sort of information Luke might have provided. Well, I guess that isn't accurate either; he did tell me that Luke told him about the two best friends Darlene went to the concert with, and that they were underage and got in with fake IDs, but he didn't really tell me if Luke had a theory as to who might have killed Darlene or if Brick had told him who he suspected."

Tony slowly added the garlic he'd been chopping to the butter sauce. "And you think that Brick had confided in Luke?"

"I think he might have. Luke and Brick were friends. They had been for a long time. They were friends back when Brick's sister was murdered. They both would have been close to her. It makes sense that Brick would have spoken to Luke about his investigation."

Tony laid huge shrimp carefully in the pan and then covered the whole thing with a sturdy lid. "So you think that Luke gave Mike something that could point him toward the killer, and he failed to share this with you during your brief conversation?"

I nodded. "Yes. That is exactly what I am saying."

"And this has you upset?"

"Of course I'm upset. Mike knows I am interested in this case."

"So even though Mike is the cop and you are a civilian, you believe he should share everything he knows with you?"

I could sense that Tony's annoying questions were leading to a point, so I asked him what it was he was trying to tell me.

"I seem to remember you telling me that you planned to stay out of things and let Mike do his job."

"I did say that."

"But I am sensing that you didn't really mean it."

I let out a breath. "I wanted to mean it, but I'm not good at hanging back and waiting it out on the sidelines. If there is a murder to solve—or any mystery to solve, for that matter—I find that I need to be right there on the front lines. It might just possibly be in my DNA."

Tony chuckled. He handed me a glass of wine. "Now that I totally believe. Maybe Mike isn't trying to keep anything from you. Maybe he knew you were in a hurry, so he just didn't get into everything."

"I was in a hurry, and I guess I was the one to end the conversation by telling him that I needed to go."

"So maybe you should call him and check in with him," Tony suggested. "After we eat. The scampi will be ready as soon as I boil the spaghetti. There is a salad in the refrigerator if you want to grab it. The dressing is on the door."

"Should I put the bread in the oven?"

"I was going to wait to heat it until the pasta is almost done. I have fresh Parmesan grated if you want that. It is in the Baggie in the cheese compartment."

I opened the refrigerator and grabbed the salad, dressing, and Parmesan. It was a good thing I walked so much during the course of my working day. Otherwise, Tony's cooking would make me fat. "How'd things go today with the video game?"

"Really well. We messed around with some design options today. We want the interface to be user-friendly but not *too* user-friendly. Real gamers don't want their games to be so easy that even someone inexperienced can excel."

"Yeah, I can see how a game that is challenging enough to get the attention of competitive gamers would be important. I'm sure between you and

Shaggy, you will come up with something really awesome."

Tony slipped the bread into the oven and then poured the pasta into a strainer. "I think so as well." He shook the water from the strainer and then transferred the pasta to a bowl. "Shaggy gave me a game he has to test if you want to play later."

"I'm in. In fact, I'm still on a high from beating your pants off the other night."

"You are more than welcome to beat my pants off any time you want," he said with a smile.

I threw a piece of bread at his head. "That's not what I meant."

Tony winked. "I know. I spoke to Nona today."

"Oh. How is she?"

"Good. I told her that we might try to come for a visit in the fall. She was, as predicted, very excited about the idea."

I sat down at the table after topping off my wine. "I want to meet her, of course, but I have to say that I am sort of nervous as well. Does she speak English?"

"Not a lot," Tony admitted.

"So we won't even be able to talk to each other. Could be awkward."

"You have months until the trip. I could teach you some basic phrases in Italian. Enough so you could get by."

I served myself a tongful of salad. "I'd like that. Very much. I've never learned another language. But it seems difficult."

"Not really. Every language has rules to follow. Once you understand those rules, you can get by. We'll start with some easy phrases and build on that."

"Okay. I'm willing to try. How long do you want to visit for?"

"Maybe three weeks? Less if you can't get the time off work, but Italy is beautiful in the fall. I think that once you get there, you'll want to have as much time as can be arranged."

Three weeks. What if Nona hated me? Three weeks seemed like a long time, but Tony had done a ton of favors for me, and he never asked for anything in return. I supposed I could endure whatever I needed to if it was going to make him happy. "We should pick dates soon, but I think I can manage three weeks."

"Maybe we can leave the end of September and be back in plenty of time for Halloween. Why don't you check with your supervisor about any vacation limitations and I'll check my schedule, and we'll settle on dates in the next couple of weeks?"

"Will we go to Rome?" I'd always wanted to see Rome.

"Of course. You can't go to Italy and not go to Rome. We can do anything you want to do."

"Venice. I've always wanted to go to Venice."

It wasn't until later, after we'd eaten and the kitchen was clean, that Tony shared with me the rest of his news. The news he wasn't even sure he wanted to share but knew I would be angry with him for not sharing if he didn't.

"I got a call from one of the men from the CIA who came by the other night. He told me that he has reason to believe that your father has returned to Montana. He wants us to try to track him down and then fill them in on his location."

I frowned. "That doesn't seem right. Were you ever able to confirm that they really are CIA?"

Tony nodded. "I checked, and they are. But I agree that something seems off. It isn't at all like the CIA to enlist the help of civilians. It is true that we have had some success in tracking him down in the past, and I can even see why they feel he might be here to try to connect with you."

I raised a brow. "Connect with me? They think he is going to try to contact me?"

Tony nodded. "That seems to be their theory."

"Why would he do that? He went to a lot of trouble to make me think he was dead. Why would he just show up here after all these years?"

"I guess they figured that he knows we have been looking for him and might have decided to make contact to stop the searches. Or perhaps they think he needs something from you, or even possibly from me. Maybe your trip to the lake alerted him to the fact that you had been provided with part of the story and he wants to fill in the blanks. I really don't know why he might contact you, but they seem to think that contacting you is the reason he is in Montana. They want to use you as bait, but they also want to be sure you notify them right away if he tries to make contact."

I stood up and began to pace around the room. "No way. If my dad contacts me, I am going to hear what he has to say. There is no way I am going to tell these men, whose intentions are completely undetermined." I looked at Tony. "Should we try to get a message to him? To let him know the CIA is after him?"

"Get a message to him how?"

I paused to think about it. "I'm not sure. I suppose he might be watching us the same way we are watching him. If this were a movie, there would be some sort of dark web chat room where we could leave a message."

"That actually might not be a bad idea. It does seem like your dad might be watching us, although for the chat room idea to work, we'd need to find a way to let him know what we are doing. Maybe we could post a cryptic message to social media. Let me work on it and see what I can come up with."

"Okay. In the meantime, I think I'll call Mike to see what he might know about Brick's murder that he hasn't shared yet. If he doesn't feel inclined to do it now, I won't push it."

Unfortunately, Mike didn't answer his cell, so I had to be content with leaving a message. I wondered once again if I should tell him that Dad could very well be right here in Montana and that the CIA might be looking for him. On one hand, I was afraid that he would totally overreact; on the other, if he was keeping a secret like that from me and I eventually found out about it, I was sure that I'd be madder than a cat in a bathtub. Was I willing to risk my relationship with Mike on the off chance that doing so might protect my father, whose motives I still didn't understand completely?

Chapter 13

Wednesday, March 27

By the time Wednesday rolled around, I still hadn't decided what I was going to do about Mike. Should I tell him what was going on with the CIA and their search for Dad? Should I let him know that Dad had been in Montana as recently as last week? Should I push to find out what he knew about Brick's murder, or should I just let it go and allow him to do his job? He had returned my call the previous day and seemed intentionally vague about Brick's murder, which I had to admit I found irritating. Part of me wanted to keep the information about Dad from him the same way he appeared to be keeping information about Brick from me, but his information was connected with his job and mine was personal to us both. Perhaps I should sit him down and try to share what I could. But it would be just like Mike to recognize the CIA guys as fellow law enforcement and give them everything we had. And if Mike did side with the CIA, would he be right in doing so? Were Tony and I wrong in our basic mistrust of the men? Lordy B, this was complicated.

In fact, the uncertainty of the whole thing was making me just a tiny bit crazy, so when Bree invited me for drinks after work, I jumped on it. In my mind, even wedding planning catastrophes, which I assumed were behind the invite, would be better than obsessing over Brick's murder or whether or not to fill Mike in on the updates regarding our dad.

"Thanks for meeting me," Bree said as I slid into a booth at one of our favorite bars.

"No problem. What's up? It's not the venue?"

Bree shook her head. "It's not the venue. It's not even the wedding, for that matter. It's Mike."

"Mike?"

Bree looked uncertain. She hesitated, appeared to reconsider even talking to me, and then finally said, "I'm not sure I should say anything. Mike is my fiancé and I know I should keep his confidences. It's just that things have seemed odd the past few days."

"Odd?"

"Maybe *odd* is an odd word to use."

I took a sip of my drink. "Just start at the beginning and tell me what you are trying so hard not to tell me but clearly want to."

Bree sighed. "A couple of nights ago, Mike and I were at dinner. This man walked in and asked to speak to him privately. Mike got up and followed him out into the parking lot. They talked for maybe ten minutes and then Mike came back inside. I asked him what that was all about, and he just said that the guy had a tip about one of the cases he was working on and wanted to deliver it in private. I didn't think much about it at first. Mike is a cop, and he does receive tips from sources who don't want to speak to him in an official capacity. I continued to chat on about the caterer for the reception, but then I realized that Mike wasn't listening to a thing I was saying. I called him on it and he apologized and made a real effort to pay attention."

"And?" I knew there had to be more to the story.

"And after dinner he took me home. I assumed he'd come in, but he said he needed to get home. He never turns down the chance to *come in*, if you know what I mean."

I did.

"He seemed to be distracted, so I said my goodbyes and let it go. The thing is, he has seemed distracted ever since. It has been several days now, and he still hasn't wanted to *come in*."

Okay, that *was* odd. "Do you think that whatever is going on has something to do with the man who pulled him outside?"

"I don't know for sure, but that was definitely when it started."

"What did the guy look like?"

Bree shrugged. "Tall. Dark hair. Clean shaven."

"What was he wearing?"

"Dress pants and a dress shirt. No tie or jacket, but he looked like he could be a professional of some sort who'd discarded his tie and jacket on his way home from work."

"And what day did you say this was?"

Bree frowned. "I guess it was Friday."

Men in White Eagle, even professionals, tended to dress down, which made me suspect that the man who'd pulled Mike aside might not have been from around here. The men from the CIA looking for Dad had shown up at Tony's on Wednesday, and then he got the call from them on Monday. Could they have been in town watching us all this time? Could they have figured out who Mike was and asked for his cooperation as well? One thing was for sure: I definitely needed to speak to him.

"Did Mike say anything at all about who the guy might have been or which case he gave him the tip regarding?"

"No. I've asked him several times if something is wrong, or if the man who pulled him aside said something to upset him, and he just assures me that everything is fine. I want to believe him, but he doesn't seem fine."

"I'll talk to Mike," I offered. "It is probably nothing, but I know that it is important to Mike not to bring work home. He wants his time with you to be about the two of you and not his job. His reluctance to talk about it might be nothing more than that."

Bree smiled. "You think so?"

I nodded. "I do."

"That's actually kind of sweet."

"Mike is a sweet guy, although as the woman who is marrying him, I'm sure you know that."

Bree placed her hand over mine. "I do know that. And thank you. I don't know why I'm making such a big deal about this. Mike works hard. He has an important job. Sometimes he is going to be distracted. Even too distracted to *come in* after our date. I really need to learn to stop obsessing over his every mood."

"You will. With time. I think the whole wedding thing has introduced an element of stress into both your lives. Once you are married, it will all be over and you can relax."

Bree frowned. "Do you know how ridiculous that sounds?"

I raised a brow. "Ridiculous?"

"You are totally right. This wedding is causing us both quite a bit of angst. And why? I love Mike. I want to build a life with him. Why on earth am I obsessing over the details of the ceremony and the reception?"

"I told you to relax and enjoy it." *About a million times*, I added in my mind.

"You did, and I should." Bree let out a little sigh. "I will. I'm going to make this as easy on Mike as I can as well. Who cares if we have a dream wedding or we get married at a drive-through chapel in Vegas? The point is that we will be married."

"Exactly. Although as fun as the drive-through chapel sounds, Mom will literally kill you if you elope. But I agree with the rest. Take a step back and enjoy the journey."

I'd left Tilly with Tony, who had come into town with Titan to hang out with Shaggy, so I decided to head in that direction. When I arrived at the comic book and video game store Shaggy owned, I found them in the middle of a heated battle with a cluster of postapocalyptic spider soldiers. One of the coolest things about Shaggy's store is that he has a gaming area in the back where customers can try out the various video games he features each month. The store was closed, but that didn't prevent Tony and Shaggy from taking advantage of the comfy seating and large screen in the preview room.

"How'd it go?" Tony asked without missing a beat in his quest to rid the world of the eight-legged army.

"Okay." I greeted both dogs. "Bree just had some things on her mind that she wanted help working through. I can see the two of you are right in the middle of important world-saving maneuvers. Should I order us a pizza?"

Tony hit Pause on the game. "No. Shaggy has a woman waiting for him at home, so we were about to quit anyway. We can grab a bite on the way back to my place."

Okay, that caught my interest. Shaggy was a nice guy, but he didn't really date a lot, and I had never known him to live with anyone. "A woman?"

"Her name is Mari," Shaggy provided.

"And she is living with you?"

Shaggy nodded. "For now. We met at a gaming convention two years ago. She lived in Seattle at the time, but we've kept in touch, so when she lost her job, I invited her to come here and help me run the store. I figure that once Tony and I really get into the development of the game, I'll need the extra help. Mari hasn't found a place to live yet, so she is staying with me."

I wasn't sure if *staying with me* meant that she was sleeping on his sofa or sleeping in his bed, but I didn't figure it was any of my business and it would be rude to ask. "I'd love to meet her. Maybe the four of us can get together for dinner this weekend."

Shaggy turned off the game and began cleaning up a bit. "I'd like for you to meet her. I'll ask her." Shaggy glanced at Tony, who had stood up and was putting on his jacket. "So, are you on for Friday?"

Tony nodded. "I'll be here."

"Be here?" I asked Tony as we called to Titan and Tilly and headed out into the parking lot.

"Shaggy has a potential investor for our game he wants me to meet. I told him I would chat with the guy, who will be in town on Friday."

"I wasn't aware that you were planning to take on investors."

"I didn't know that finding investors was part of Shaggy's plan either, but it isn't a bad idea. It can complicate things a bit, though, so I want to meet the guy and then decide if I think he is someone I can work with. If not, I'm sure Shaggy will understand. This project was his idea, so I want him to feel like he has a say in how we proceed, but I am the one putting up most of the money, and I'll need to be comfortable with the decisions we make as well." Tony glanced at Tilly. "Why don't you take the dogs home and I'll stop to grab the pizza?"

"Sounds good. I'll toss together a salad to go with it."

I let my mind drift to my conversation with Bree as Titan, Tilly, and I drove out to Tony's. I considered how to approach him about the incident without letting him know that Bree was upset about the encounter and Mike's ensuing mood, and without spilling the fact that she had spoken to me about it, which would be a betrayal of trust. I also wondered if bringing it up wouldn't just be opening a can of worms if it turned out that the man who'd pulled Mike aside was just providing a tip and didn't have a thing to do with Dad or the men from the CIA who were looking for him. I supposed my best bet at this point would be to talk things over with Tony before I did anything. He had an objective way of looking at things that escaped me at times when it came to my family.

Once I arrived at Tony's, I let the dogs out to run around for a few minutes before going inside to check on the cats. When they were snuggled and fed, I went upstairs to change into something more comfortable. If I was going to stay out at Tony's for the entire spring and summer, I was going to have to bring more of my clothes here, but for now, soft gray and navy-blue sweatshirts would work just fine.

I thought about Shaggy's live-in employee as I tossed the salad. I assumed that Tony had met her, so I'd have to ask him about her when he got home. I considered Shaggy a close friend and would love to see him in a relationship, but his history with women wasn't all that stellar, so I was worried that he'd end up getting hurt. Not that it was my job to worry about his love life, but I supposed I was the sort to worry about all my friends to a certain degree.

By the time I'd made the salad, Tony had pulled up in the drive. I set out plates and grabbed a couple of beers. "I'm starving," I said as he placed the box with the extra-large pie on the table.

"I worked up a bit of an appetite battling the spider army as well."

I laughed. "I bet you and Shaggy are going to have a blast developing your game. And remember, I'm your number one tester."

"Of course. It'll be a while before we have anything to test, but once we do, you will be first in line."

I slipped into a chair and served myself a helping of salad. "So tell me about this Mari. I assume you've met her?"

Tony slipped a slice of pizza onto his plate. "Sure. Lots of times. In fact, I was at the convention when Shaggy and I met her and her friend Ivy two years ago."

I raised a brow. "I see. Are we talking about a double date sort of situation?"

Tony nodded. "At the time, yes."

"Should I be jealous?" Okay, I already was.

"Absolutely not. I haven't stayed in touch with Ivy the way Shaggy has with Mari, although she does send me an email every now and then. But we're just friends. Even at the time of the convention, it was more that the four of us hung out during the week, and during that time we established a friendship. When the convention ended, Shaggy arranged to stay in contact with Mari, but I couldn't wait to get home to you."

I crossed my arms over my chest. "Me? We weren't even dating two years ago."

Tony placed his hand over mine. "It is true that I'd yet to win you over with my rugged good looks and boyish charm, but the truth of the matter is, I'd been biding my time, waiting for your feelings for me to catch up with my feelings for you since we first met in middle school."

Aw. That was so sweet. I squeezed Tony's hand. "Sorry it took so long."

Tony shrugged. "That's okay. You were worth waiting for."

I took a sip of my beer. "So, about Mari. Are she and Shaggy... friends?"

"Yes, they are friends, and yes, they are more than friends. If I know you as well as I think I do, I know that you are probably worried that Shaggy will get hurt. But honestly, I don't think he will. Mari is a really awesome person, and quite frankly, I think she is perfect for Shaggy."

I felt myself relax just a bit. "That's good. I can't wait to meet her."

"I'll follow up with Shaggy about the dinner idea. In the meantime, I think she will be at the store training this week. You should stop by."

"I might just do that. If I can find a spare minute. It seems like I have fallen behind on my route every day for the past week at least."

"You've been preoccupied with Brick's murder. Any news?"

I shook my head. "I was going to try to talk to Mike today, but I didn't have a chance. The last couple of times I've called him, he's seemed evasive, which is sort of strange because he seemed to be willing to talk to me about the investigation in the beginning."

"I suppose that Mike has a lot on his mind. He might just be preoccupied."

I supposed that could be true. "The CIA guys who stopped by that night... Do you remember what they looked like?"

Tony paused and looked at me. "I only saw the one guy, the passenger who got out of the car. He was tall with dark hair. He wore a suit, which made him look like a fish out of water here in White Eagle. I remember thinking that he should trade out his designer threads for jeans and a sweatshirt if he wanted to blend in."

"Maybe he didn't want to blend in. Maybe intimidation was more his thing."

"I suppose you might have a point. I know I would have taken him less seriously if he'd dressed down. Why the interest in what he looked like?"

I filled Tony in on my conversation with Bree.

Tony frowned. "I can understand why the men from the CIA contacted me. I'd been actively looking for the man who used to go by the name of Grant Thomas, so they had every reason to believe that I knew he was alive. But Mike? It seems like a big risk to talk to him when they had no way of knowing if he even knew his father was still alive."

I narrowed my gaze. "That's true. Maybe this guy really was just providing Mike with a tip about one of his cases. I hadn't stopped to think about how unlikely it was that the CIA would pull Mike away from dinner when they couldn't know what sort of reaction they were going to get."

"Unless Mike had contacted them after we filled him in on what we had uncovered," Tony added.

"Well, yes, I guess there is that possibility to consider. Still, my gut is telling me not to bring it up with Mike right now. If the man who pulled Mike aside was connected with Dad's disappearance, it seems like he would have brought it up to me. The fact that he hasn't indicates in my mind that the guy was after something else." I paused and thought about things. "I don't like keeping anything from Mike, but I don't know how he would react if he did know the CIA was after Dad. Best to keep the situation between the two of us at least for the time being."

Chapter 14

Friday, March 29

On Friday morning I found myself actually ahead of schedule for the first time in a long time, so I decided to stop by the police station to check in with Mike.

"Morning, Frank. Is Mike in?"

"In his office."

I instructed Tilly to wait with Frank and Leonard, then headed down the hallway. I found Mike sitting in his chair staring into space. "Seems like you might have something heavy on your mind."

Mike looked at me. "I do. Have a seat."

I sat down across from him. I assumed this had to do with our father, but it turned out that his solemn expression was about Brick's murder.

"I just spoke to Lacy Tilton, who I have been trying to get ahold of ever since Luke Warner gave me her name. If you remember, she was one of the two friends Darlene Brannigan went to the concert with on the night she died."

"Yes, I remember. Did she know something that might help you with your search for Brick's killer?"

"She told me that on the night Darlene died she had persuaded both Ginny and her to attend the concert with her so that she could meet up with someone she had met at a club the night before."

"Club? I thought Darlene was only sixteen?"

"She was, but she had a fake ID."

I nodded. "That's right. Go on."

"Lacy didn't know the name of the man that Darlene planned to connect with, but she did say that she had indicated that he was with a band. She wasn't sure if he was a musician or a support person, such as a roadie, but she did say that the name of the band was Satan's Sin."

I wrinkled my nose. "Sounds lovely," I said with a hint of sarcasm.

"They were definitely not for everyone. The thing I found interesting was that the four band members went by the names Lucifer, Beelzebub, Satan, and Abaddon."

"All names for the devil."

"Exactly. And it just so happens the first letter of each of those names, L, B, S, and A, coincide with the letters used to identify the four DNA samples Brick sent for testing."

My eyes grew large. "So, if the killer was L, Lucifer did it."

"That would be my guess."

"So how did Brick get DNA samples from all four men?"

"That I do not know. The band is currently doing a reunion tour, so I suppose Brick might have attended one of their concerts and then followed them around until he was able to collect what he needed. As the owner of a bar who hires bands to play on Friday and Saturday nights, he could even have had an in with the band's manager."

"So now what?"

"The band is doing a gig in Cheyenne this weekend. I thought I might take a drive down there to try to collect my own DNA samples. If I can prove what it seems Brick proved—that Lucifer was Darlene's killer—I think we should be able to put both murder cases to bed."

"Cheyenne is a fifteen-hour drive. Let me call Tony. Maybe his friend with the jet can fly us all down there."

"All?"

"You will need help collecting the samples. If Tony's friend is free, he should be able to fly us down this evening after we both get off work. I'll book a hotel for Tony and me and you and Bree, if she wants to go. I'll see if Tony can snag us some backstage passes, which will allow us to collect items that might possess the DNA we need."

Mike hesitated.

"It's a good plan."

"Do you think Tony can get the passes?"

I nodded. "He knows a lot of people. I'll call him now, and if the jet is free, I'll check with Shaggy to see if he can stay out at Tony's to look after the animals."

Chapter 15

Saturday, March 30

As it turned out, Tony's pilot friend was available, Tony did know someone and was able to get us concert tickets and backstage passes, and Shaggy and Mari were happy to stay out at Tony's to look after the animals. Mike, Bree, Tony, and I all flew to Cheyenne on Friday evening, arriving just in time to check into our hotel and head off to bed. It turned out that the concert was a multiband event that started at four in the afternoon and ran until after midnight. The four of us dressed casually in torn jeans and leather so as not to stand out in the crowd. The plan was to identify the four members of the band and then split up into pairs, following each member until we had DNA samples from all of them. Mike had outfitted each of us with backpacks, rubber gloves, and evidence bags. Trying to slip on one of the gloves without being noticed was not going to be easy, but I figured we'd work out the details as we went along.

While the music wasn't the sort I enjoyed, I found the atmosphere energetic and somewhat alluring. While I was pretty sure that at least part of the reason the energy level was so high was due to the drugs that were circulating quite openly, I still found the liveliness of the place invigorating.

"Okay," Mike said before we separated. "We know what we need to do. It will be important that we collect our samples without drawing attention to ourselves, so blend in. Once you have a sample, text the others to let us know what you have. Remember, anything with saliva is best. Discarded gum, a cigarette butt, a discarded glass, or a beer bottle. If at all possible, we should try to collect more than one sample per person, but we don't want to overdo it and become obvious. The band member who goes by the name Lucifer is our prime suspect. If nothing else, we need a viable sample from him. We'll regroup after a couple of hours so we can evaluate our progress."

Once Mike had finished his spiel, he and Bree went off in one direction and Tony and I went in another. Having access to the VIP tent was going to be the key to our success. Sometimes I forgot how connected my easygoing boyfriend really was.

"This is actually kind of fun," I said to Tony as we mingled with the crowd, keeping an eye out for any of our four subjects.

"I will admit that doing the detective thing is sort of a rush. And while I'm not really a fan of this music, I'm kind of getting into it. At least for today."

"Yeah, I know what you mean. I'm sure I will have a splitting headache by the end of the day, but right now I am feeling the vibe." I paused and looked around at the crowd. Mike had acquired a list of all five bands that were scheduled to play, and Tony had downloaded recent photos of the members of each one. So far, I had only been able to identify two musicians, and neither were from Satan's Sin. "I hope the band members show up at some point. If all they do is go onstage, do their set, and leave, this whole trip will have been a waste of time."

Tony took my hand in his. "I think they'll show. But even if they don't, it won't have been a waste. Sometimes these things take time."

I supposed Tony was right. "There is one thing I've been wondering now that we are here."

"What's that?" Tony asked.

"If Darlene left in the middle of the concert and was never seen alive again, she couldn't have been meeting up with one of the four members of the band. They were all onstage. If her intention was to meet up with one of them, why wouldn't she have just waited until after the concert?"

"Good question," Tony acknowledged. "Maybe she figured she wouldn't be able to get away from her friends after the concert, or maybe she arranged for someone else—maybe one of Lucifer's friends—to take her backstage to wait for the band to finish."

"Lacy seemed to know that Darlene wanted to go to the concert to hook up with someone associated with the band. That brings me to the question of why Lacy lied about the fact that Darlene was at the concert to hook up with a man when she was interviewed two decades ago, and why Darlene lied about going to find the bathroom. Why not just tell her friends what she was doing if they knew about the hookup?"

Tony frowned. "Where are you going with this?"

"I'm just wondering if we aren't barking up the wrong tree. Not that I don't think we should try to obtain DNA from the band members as planned, but I feel like we are missing something important. The problem is, I have no idea what that something might be."

Tony nudged my arm. "It looks like Abaddon just entered the tent. Let's hang back, but keep an eye on him. He's heading toward the bar. Hopefully, that will result in a used glass or beer bottle."

The problem, we soon found, was that glass was not allowed at the concert, so what we ended up with was a plastic cup. I wasn't sure if DNA could be pulled from plastic, but as soon as the cup was abandoned, Tony did the supersleuth thing and managed to bag it and slip it into his backpack. We texted Mike, who informed us that he had managed to get a cigarette butt that Satan had tossed, which meant we needed to hope that Lucifer and Beelzebub showed up.

"What if the samples we collect are no good?" I asked Tony.

"The band has three more stops on their tour. We can try again. If we can match the samples we are collecting with any of the samples Brick had, that at least would let us know we are on the right track."

"All of these men have black hair. It may be dyed black, but it is black nonetheless," I pointed out. "Mike said from the police report that the hair found in Darlene's hand was blond. I suppose that one or more of the men could be wearing a black wig and there is blond hair underneath, but somehow I doubt it."

"That is a really good point. I'll step out into the parking lot where the reception is better and try to pull up a photo of the band twenty years ago. Maybe the black hair is a recent adaptation."

"I'll come with you. I really don't want to stay here alone."

We left the tent and went out into the parking area. Tony pulled up a photo of an album cover from 2002. All four musicians had black hair. That was five years after Darlene was murdered, though, so Tony continued to search until he found a promotional poster from 1996. Three of the men had black hair then, but one of them, the drummer Beelzebub, was blond. The sample that matched the old DNA had been labeled with the letter L, however, which seemed to indicate that it belonged to Lucifer. Something wasn't making sense.

"Let's head back inside," Tony said.

I started coughing when we returned to the tent. I hadn't noticed the strong stench of marijuana when we'd been inside before. I had a feeling I was going to be stoned by the end of the night from secondhand smoke if I spent too much more time in the VIP area.

"There's Lucifer," I whispered to Tony. "He is heading toward the men's room."

"I'll follow him," Tony offered.

Which meant I was going to be alone, so I texted Mike to check in and to see how he and Bree were doing. Mike texted back to say that while he hadn't managed to track down any additional band members, he had run into a big-time groupie who seemed to have all the scoop about the history of the band, including the names of all the various roadies who had toured with them over the years. Bree pretended to be representing a popular music blog, and she was happily spilling her guts about everything she knew.

By the time I finished texting with Mike, Tony had returned.

"Did you get anything?"

Tony nodded. "I did."

I couldn't help but make a face. "Dare I ask?"

"A tissue. Lucifer blew his nose, then tossed the tissue in the trash, and I used my gloves and a Baggie to secure it. Now we just need a sample from Beelzebub."

"I don't see him." I stood on tiptoe and looked around.

"Yeah. I don't either. I guess if he doesn't show before they take the stage, we'll just need to wait until after their set and hope they come back to the tent."

Beelzebub still hadn't visited the VIP tent by the time the band went on, so the four of us left the area to see the concert. The group was loud, that was for certain, but they really weren't too bad, and their lyrics were actually haunting if you could get past all the noise. I focused on the face of each of the men as they played. They seemed to be having a good time, but I noticed a look of fatigue as well. If I had to guess, they had been partying hard the entire weekend.

"I think my hearing is going to be permanently affected," Bree shouted.

"I agree," I shouted back. "Do you want to walk over to the beer tent and take a break?"

Bree nodded.

I told Tony what we were going to do, and Bree filled Mike in on our plans. The music could still be heard quite far away at the concession area, but at least we could speak without shouting.

"Dang it, I stepped in gum," Bree said.

"Sorry. I saw that guy who was in line in front of us toss it on the ground. I should have warned you. Hang on and I'll see if I can get it off." I pulled out a pair of gloves and pried it from the bottom of Bree's shoe. I was about to toss it in the trash when, at the last minute, I put it in one of our sample bags.

"Why are you saving the gum?" Bree asked.

I shrugged. "I'm not sure. The guy who tossed the gum looked familiar. I can't quite place him, but something is telling me to hang on to it."

Bree looked toward the edge of the tent that opened onto a passageway that led to the rear of the stage. "I think the guy is with the band. He headed down that hallway that is restricted to band members and their teams."

"Before we leave today, let's see if we can find out what his name is. I just have this gut feeling that he might come into play at some point."

Bree bit the corner of her lip. "Do you think he was with the band all those years ago?"

"I don't know. Maybe. He looked old enough to have been with them for a long time. The groupie you met gave you a bunch of names. Do any of them who have been with the band since the 1990s begin with an L?"

Bree pulled out the list. "The band manager is named Barry. He has been with them from the beginning. The publicist is Arnie, and he has been around since the beginning as well. The woman also knew the real names of the band members."

"Which are?"

"Satan's real name is Roy, Lucifer's is Ben, Beelzebub's is Lance, and Abaddon's is Tyson."

"So if Brick was going by real names rather than stage names, L could be Lance, who we know as Beelzebub."

"Yeah, I guess. I suppose identifying the killer is really going to come down to the DNA. Without that, I can't see how we'll ever figure this out."

Bree and I made it to the front of the line for the beer. We ordered four cups, then headed back to where Tony and Mike were waiting for us. Each group played a set that lasted an hour to ninety minutes, and then there was a short intermission while the next band set up. At first, I was afraid that Satan's Sin would leave after their set, but we heard someone mention that all the bands took the stage at the end for one huge grand finale.

After Satan's Sin completed their set, the four of us returned to the VIP tent, which by this point was almost as loud as the concert itself. We had samples from three of the four band members; all we needed was Beelzebub's, which, given the fact that he had been the only one of the four with blond hair, whose real name was Lance, and who was at the top of my suspect list, was the most important.

"Do we know what some of the others who might have been around back then look like?" I asked. "The band manager, for example? It seems that as long as we are here, we may as well collect as much DNA as we can."

"I think the guy over there is the manager," Tony said.

I considered the man Tony had referred to. He had on a simple red T-shirt, faded jeans, and Nikes. He didn't look like a band manager. Of course, I didn't know any band managers, so how could I say?

"Who's he talking to?" I asked.

"I think that is the head roadie," Mike said. "Both men have been with the band since the beginning. And I agree that it wouldn't hurt to try to collect DNA for them as well. Let's watch them and wait for an opening."

"I just hope Beelzebub shows soon. I really don't want to have to hang around until midnight when the band will be back for their encore," I replied.

"Other than onstage, I haven't seen him at all," Mike said. "I'll ask around, see if I can find out whether he tends to hang out with the fans."

As it turned out, Beelzebub wasn't the sort to mingle. Mike spoke to several fans who followed the band, and everyone pretty much agreed that Beelzebub headed back to his trailer between sets.

"I'll see if I can track him down," Mike said. "The rest of you should stay here and focus on getting DNA samples from the manager and anyone else you can track down who might have been with the band when Darlene was murdered."

Mike was lucky and found Beelzebub smoking a cigarette while sitting on a bench outside his trailer. When he tossed the butt into the dirt, Mike was there to retrieve it. Tony managed to bag a cup that the band manager had been drinking from, and Bree was able to pick up a napkin that the head roadie had used to wipe his mouth from the trash. By the time we left, we had samples from eight men. Now we just had to hope that one of them would give us a match.

Chapter 16

Friday, April 6

It was a week since we'd collected our DNA samples and Mike finally received the results.

"I can't believe that none of the items we collected matched the sample Brick had for subject L," I groaned.

"We were wrong about the whole thing," Mike informed me. "None of the samples that Brick tested matched any of the four band members. Two samples we took did match Brick's: the one for the band manager, Barry Boxer, matched the sample for B and the one for Arnie Cook, the publicist, matched the sample for A. Neither matched the original sample that was found with Darlene's body."

"So we still need to figure out who L and S are," I said. "Did you test the gum?"

"Gum?" Mike asked.

"The gum that I pried off the bottom of Bree's shoe. I put it into one of the sample bags. I'm pretty sure that the guy who tossed it onto the ground was with the band."

"I'm sorry, but I didn't notice any gum. Did you label it?"

"No," I admitted.

"I'll go back to look through all of them again. We had multiple samples for some of the suspects, so rather than testing them all, I picked out the best ones for testing. The gum could be in the pile I didn't use. Do you happen to know the name of the guy whose gum Bree stepped on?"

"No, but he looked familiar. I might have seen him in one of the photos we looked at when we were checking out the band members."

"Okay, then take another look at the photos to see if you can identify him. Maybe we'll luck out and his name will begin with an L or a S."

"Do you have the photos?" I asked.

"Frank has the file up front. He can show them to you. If you do identify the guy, text me. I need to head out for a meeting with Dover. He claims to have information to share, so I figured I'd listen."

"Why would he wait until now to tell you what he knows?"

Mike shrugged. "Sometimes folks have to work up to doing what they've known all along they should."

I followed Mike down the hallway. He left the station, and I asked Frank if I could take a look at the file. I needed to get back to my route and didn't have a lot of time, but I thought I ought to take a quick look now and then come back for a better one later if need be.

The photos were mostly ones of the band that Mike had found from old magazines, album covers, publicity flyers, and internet searches. Some of them were only of the band members, while others were of live concerts that included people in the audience.

"Do you know if there is a photo of the concert that Darlene attended the night she died?" I asked.

"I don't think so. Mike has been printing photos as he finds them, but I'm sure if he had one of that concert, he would have marked it. Social media nowadays pretty much guarantees that every event is captured by someone, but years ago, it wasn't as common to have concert photos as widespread as they are now."

"True. Still, it couldn't hurt to look." I called Tony and asked him to try to hunt up any photos he could find of the concert Darlene had attended the day she died. He promised to do so, and I went on with my route.

I was just leaving Grandma Hattie's Bakeshop when I got a text from Mike, asking me to find a quiet place to talk and call him when I got there. It was another nice day and Tilly and I weren't all that far from the park, so we headed in that direction.

"What's up?" I asked Mike as I settled on a bench in the sun.

"Dover told me that he went to the bar on Saturday to try to talk to Brick. Initially, he'd said he hadn't seen Brick since he'd been fired, but he was feeling guilty about the lie and wanted to clear the air."

"Do you think he might have killed Brick?"

"Honestly, no. If he had, he would never have admitted to lying. I think he realized that he would be a suspect and panicked when I asked him about the last time he'd spoken to Brick. We chatted for quite a while, and I didn't get the vibe that he was the one who pulled the trigger. He did have some information I found interesting, though."

"Oh, and what was that?"

"Dover said there was a postal box on the bar when he went in on Saturday. Brick had been looking into it but stopped when Dover walked into the empty bar. He told me there were photos laid out on the bar that Brick picked up and put somewhere behind it as Dover approached."

"It sounds like the box Brick received on the day before he died. We need to find those photos."

"I agree. I'm going to head over to the bar to take another look around. If Dover is correct and Brick had the box before opening on Saturday and was shot shortly after closing that same day, it stands to reason that the photos that were in it are still hidden somewhere in the bar."

I knew I should continue with my route and not take the time to get involved, but I could just deliver to the businesses between the park and the bar on the way, and I was ahead of schedule despite my stops to talk to Mike. "I'm heading in that direction. I'll meet you there."

As always, I felt bad when I needed to execute the drop-and-run, but today it was absolutely necessary, so I quickly apologized to each of my customers and sped through my route at what felt like record speed.

"So, now that we know we are looking for photos, that should help us focus. We didn't find any photos in the safe or on Brick's desk. He was standing at the bar looking at them when Dover came in, so maybe he stashed them somewhere near the bar."

"Makes sense." Mike walked in that direction. He bent down and began opening and closing drawers.

"I wonder if Brick had a cash drop."

Mike paused and looked at me. "You mean somewhere he could drop large bills without having to leave his position behind the bar?"

"Yeah. He'd want to be able to drop large bills rather than leaving them in the cash register." I stood in front of the register now, then looked carefully at the drawers and cabinets around me. Just beneath the register, in one cabinet, I found a faux panel that led to an opening that looked a lot like a mail slot. "I think I found it." I ran my hand down the cabinet. "If I had to guess, the panel on the bottom opens to a locked drawer." I pulled the panel aside to confirm my theory. "Of course it's locked."

Mike knelt down next to me. He studied the lock for a moment, then went into the office. I followed him and watched him open the safe we'd broken into previously and take out a ring with keys on it. I then followed him back out to the bar, where he began trying keys one after another. Eventually, the drawer opened, and sure enough, we found a pile of hundred-dollar bills piled atop a stack of photos. Mike picked up the photos and laid them out on the bar.

"These look like they were taken at a concert," I said. "I was just telling Frank we needed to look for photos of the concert Darlene went to the night she died. I have Tony working on it."

Mike picked up the photos one at a time, taking a moment to study them.

"This looks like a Satan's Sin concert." He pointed to a man standing on the stage arranging a microphone. "This looks like Lucifer. The rest of the band isn't in the photo, so I am guessing this was taken prior to the music starting."

"The place is packed," I said. It seemed a band like this one could pack in what looked to be an arena-size crowd. "I wonder what Brick was looking for."

Mike set the photo he had been looking at on the bar and pointed to one of the fans in the audience. "That's Darlene Brannigan."

I felt my heart constrict as I glanced at the young girl with the huge grin on her face. To know that she would die soon afterward was almost more than I could take. "Brick must have been looking for the killer in the crowd."

Mike frowned. "Yeah. He must have had a hunch, because he sent out the DNA samples long before he would have sent for these photos. I wonder who sent them to him."

"Hard to say without a return address on the box." I paused to think about it. Chances were, Brick had requested the photos after he sent the DNA samples to Genocom but before he had received the results. Maybe he was trying to cover all his bases. "I wonder if he was looking for someone in particular."

Mike continued to look at the photos. "Two of the four samples belonged to the band manager and publicist. Brick must have had reason to suspect them. Maybe Darlene had been hanging around the band even before that day. Maybe whoever she was there to see was someone she had met before."

"Okay, say Brick knew that his sister had been to other Satan's Sin concerts, or maybe she had been to a party attended by band members. Maybe even on more than one occasion. He put together the fact that she was killed while attending the concert with the fact that she had been following someone associated with the band. It could have been a musician, but it could also have been someone connected with the band, like the manager. Maybe he wasn't sure who she had been planning to meet, so he'd been narrowing it down over time."

"The murder occurred twenty years ago," Mike pointed out. "For Brick to be actively researching it now, something must have occurred recently to cause him to gather the DNA samples."

Mike had a point. There must have been a fairly recent event that instigated the whole thing. Something within the past year or two, if I had to guess. I supposed it was possible he had simply stumbled upon some piece of previously undiscovered evidence.

"Look at this," Mike said, setting the photo he had been looking at on the bar and pointing to a man in the crowd.

"He looks familiar."

"I'm almost certain that is Luke Warner. He is twenty years younger and he has long blond hair rather than the short brown hair he does now, but I'm sure that is him."

I squinted more closely at the photo. "Yeah, I think you are right." I looked up at Mike. "I remember that he was friends with Brick and dating Darlene when she died, but she went to the concert with friends, not him."

"According to the police report, he claimed that he was nowhere near the concert when Darlene was murdered. He provided an alibi, and the police were able to verify it."

"It appears he lied. Maybe whoever was his alibi lied as well." My eyes grew wide. "Luke starts with an L, and L's DNA matched the killer's. Do you think Luke could have murdered Darlene?"

"Maybe," Mike said. "If he was in love with Darlene and she was messing around behind his back, he could have followed her to the concert, waited for her to hook up with whoever she was there to meet, confronted her, and killed her. He might have been drunk or stoned or both at the time."

"And because he supposedly was not at the concert, he wasn't a suspect. Then, all these years later, he moved to White Eagle and resurrected his friendship with Brick. At some point, maybe he said something, or Brick saw something at his home to cause him to take another look at the case. Maybe Luke was even the one to put him on to the band manager and publicist."

"It seems I'm going to need to have a chat with Luke." Mike gathered up the photos. "Thanks for your help."

"No problem. I need to finish up my route now, but call me after you've had a chance to follow up with him."

Chapter 17

I still hadn't heard from Mike when I got home that evening. I'd called him a dozen times, but the calls went straight to voice mail. I supposed if Luke had revealed his guilt, Mike could be bogged down in arrest paperwork. Still, I hoped he'd call me. I thought about calling Bree, but if she didn't know what was going on and Mike hadn't called her to check in, she'd just worry.

"Have you heard from Mike?" I asked Tony the minute Tilly and I came through the kitchen door.

"No. Were you expecting him to call?"

I explained our trip to the bar, the concert photo, and Mike's plan to have a chat with Luke. "I've called a bunch of times, but I just get his voice mail."

"Are you worried that he ran into problems with Luke?"

"I don't know. Maybe. He is a cop and he has a gun, and I'm pretty sure he planned to bring Frank with him, but I will admit I'll feel better after I hear from him."

"Have you tried calling Frank?" Tony asked.

"No. I'll do that right now."

Like Mike, Frank didn't answer.

"Let's head over to the station. If they aren't there, we'll head to Luke's to see what is going on. I'll grab my jacket if you can let Titan out real fast."

The drive back into town seemed the longest in my life. A quick glance at the police station informed us that neither Frank nor Mike were there. We drove to Luke's house, but it was dark and seemed deserted as well.

"What now?" Tony asked.

"I wonder if we can find out where Luke was working today. It was the middle of the workday when Mike and I met at the bar, so I would be willing to bet that Mike just drove to the worksite to speak with him there."

Tony pulled up his phone. I watched as he did a search for Warner Construction, found the number, and called it. The phone rang, and eventually, the line was picked up by voice mail. "He's not answering." Tony drummed his fingers on the steering wheel. "If Mike took his squad car to talk to Luke and it is still there, we should be able to track it. Let's go back to the station."

I wasn't sure what the penalty was for breaking into a police station, but in that moment I didn't much care. The doors were all locked, but the alarm had not been set, meaning that the last person to leave hadn't planned to be gone long. Tony logged on to Mike's computer, but it was password protected.

"Maybe you should call the rookie."

"Gage," I said.

"See if he can come in."

I nodded and looked for the number. Thankfully, he answered after the third ring. He told me that Mike and Frank had both left the station a couple of hours earlier and had asked him to keep an eye on Leonard. He'd gotten hungry, so he'd packed the puppy in his car and run down the street for a burger. He promised to come right back and help us locate Mike's cruiser. As soon as he arrived, he was able to use his own computer to access the tracker on Mike's car.

"He's at that new housing development outside of town," Tony said, looking over Gage's shoulder.

I looked at Gage. "Do you have your gun?"

He nodded.

"Ever use it?"

"At the shooting range."

"Grab it." I looked at Leonard, and then at Tony. "We'll bring him with us." I turned back to Gage. "You know where we are going?"

He nodded.

"Okay, you take point. We'll want to sneak up on the place really quietly until we can assess the situation. Tony and I will be in his car right behind you. When you arrive at the road that leads to the development, pull over to the side. If for some reason things went south and Mike and Frank are in trouble, we won't want to alert Luke that we're there until we can come up with a plan."

"Okay. You can count on me."

I sure hoped so. The kid was as nice as nice could be, and he seemed sincere in his desire to be a cop, but as far as I knew, the only training he'd had was the little bit he'd received from Mike in the past few weeks. From what I'd heard, all he'd done so far was follow Mike around, answer phones, and do some filing.

As instructed, Gage pulled over to the side when we arrived at the road leading to the new development. It was almost dark, so Tony grabbed a couple of flashlights from his glove box.

"Tess and I are going to sneak around and approach from the back. Once we get our eyes on the situation, we'll call you and let you know what to do," Tony said to Gage. "You have your phone?"

Gage held it up.

"What's the number?" Tony typed it into his phone as Gage recited it. Tony looked him in the eye. "If you don't hear from me in ten minutes, come on down the road with lights and siren blazing."

Gage looked like he might pass out.

"It's okay," I said. "Just watch your phone for a text. Hopefully, we'll find the situation is under control and you will be told to stand down."

The kid, who I'd heard had just turned nineteen, took a deep breath and stood up straighter. "Okay. I'm ready to do whatever I have to do."

Tony and I walked through the forest as quickly and quietly as we could. Suddenly, I found myself wishing I'd taken the time to change out of my uniform. It was going to be filthy by the time we completed our mission. As we neared the houses on the first street, we saw the rear of Mike's car, which had been pulled around to the side of a house. I didn't see anyone or hear anything, and there was no sight of any lights. You would think if the men had been talking, they would have turned on their flashlights by now.

Tony continued forward with determined confidence and I followed. As we rounded the corner to the half-completed house where Mike's car was parked, Tony stopped suddenly.

"What is it?"

Tony looked around but didn't respond or move. I glance around Tony's body to see Frank on the ground in a pool of blood. I wanted to run toward him, but Tony grabbed my arm. He indicated wordlessly that we needed to continue to move with caution. Tony slowly moved forward until he was kneeling next to Frank. He put two fingers on his neck. I let out a sigh of relief when Tony nodded to let me know that he was alive. After checking Frank's pulse, we retreated back toward the woods. Tony took out his phone and called Gage. "Call for backup. Frank is down but alive. We are going to try to locate Mike before you come into the complex."

"Yes, sir."

Tony squatted down low and then moved toward the house that Frank was lying in front of. He slowly opened the back door and stepped inside. I followed closely. We crawled slowly through the framed-in room that would be the kitchen to the front of the house. When we arrived in the large room that would be the living area, we found both Mike and Luke on the floor, each in their own pools of blood.

Chapter 18

Saturday, April 7

"Mrs. Thomas." A man in green scrubs approached the waiting area where Mom, Aunt Ruthie, Bree, Tony, and I had been camping out, waiting for word on Mike's condition.

"Yes. I'm Lucy Thomas," Mom responded.

"I'm Dr. Brown. Your son is out of surgery and should be just fine."

Everyone let out a long breath.

"Can I see him?" Bree asked.

"Are you the fiancée?" Dr. Brown asked.

Bree nodded.

"Officer Thomas is still out, but I don't suppose it would hurt to let you peek in on him for a few minutes."

"I'm coming as well," Mom said.

The doctor waved over a nurse and instructed her to show Mom and Bree to Mike's room.

"What about the others?" I asked.

"Officer Hudson is still in surgery. I anticipate that we will know more in a couple of hours. Mr. Warner didn't make it."

I bowed my head. "Can you tell what happened?"

The doctor frowned. "It's hard to tell exactly, but based on the fact that all three men were shot, and from the description of the crime scene as told to me by my nurse, who seems to manage to get all the scoop, I would say that Mr. Warner shot Officer Hudson and then turned on Officer Thomas, who fired back at the same time."

"So Luke and my brother shot each other?"

"It would appear that way. Officer Thomas should be able to confirm or deny that theory when he wakes up."

"When will that be?" I asked.

"Not for quite a while. You should take your mother and your friend and head home to get some rest when they return."

"Thanks, but I think we'll wait here until we know Frank is going to be okay."

The doctor nodded. "I'll be sure that someone keeps you updated."

I turned to Ruthie. "I think it might be best for Mom to go home and get some rest. If we can convince her to go, will you drive her?"

"Of course, dear. Bree too, if you can convince her to leave. The poor dear looks like she is about to collapse."

"Yeah. The past few hours have been hard on her. Tony and I will stay until we hear about Frank. We'll text everyone."

I didn't expect that either Mom or Bree would leave, but somehow, Aunt Ruthie convinced them both to do so after promising to bring them back after they'd had a few hours of sleep. Once they left, I settled in with Tony to wait for news on Frank.

"This whole thing is so surreal," I said to Tony as I lay my head on his shoulder. "I suspect that the doctor was right in his theory that Luke shot Frank and Mike and Mike shot Luke, but it still feels sort of off."

"I'm sure once Gage and the crime scene guys finish their investigation, we will know more. Besides, as the doctor said, Mike should be able to fill in some of the blanks when he wakes up."

"I guess it was a good thing that we went looking for Mike. He and Frank would have bled out for sure if we hadn't found them. That housing development is pretty isolated. I doubt anyone would have found them until the work crew showed up on Monday."

"It seems like the crew should still have been there when Mike first arrived," Tony said.

"Maybe they got off early, it being Friday and all." I glanced toward the double doors leading into the surgical and intensive care units. "I hope we hear soon. The waiting is really getting to me."

Tony kissed me on the top of the head. "Yeah. Me too."

Just over two hours later, the doctor came out to let us know that Frank's condition was stable. He, like Mike, was still under, so Tony and I left to drive to his place. If nothing else, I was sure the dogs would need to go out.

Chapter 19

By Saturday afternoon, Mike and Frank were both alert and able to see visitors for a short period of time. Frank didn't remember anything after he arrived on the property, but Mike was able to confirm that they'd spoken to Luke about his presence at the concert twenty years before, and then showed him the photo they had as proof. Initially, he admitted that he was there but hadn't run into Darlene in the crowd, but when Mike informed him that he had her killer's DNA and would need to get a sample from him, he'd pulled out a gun and shot Frank. Mike had followed Luke after he began to run, but then Luke turned and fired at Mike just as he, noticing the gun pointed at him, fired at Luke. Luckily, Mike was able to deliver a fatal blow while the bullet from Luke's gun missed Mike's vital organs. He'd lost a lot of blood but would be able to go home in a few days.

I asked Mike if Luke had admitted to killing Brick, and he said he hadn't, though the fact that

Brick knew that Luke had killed his sister and must have confronted him indicated to all of us that Luke most likely had killed Brick to protect his secret. It would be better for everyone concerned if Mike was able to prove beyond a shadow of a doubt that Luke had killed Brick, but without a confession or additional evidence, doing so was unlikely.

Tony and I were on our way out of the hospital when we ran into Gage coming in. We stopped to chat for a moment. "How is the investigation going?" I asked.

Gage told me that they'd been able to confirm everything Mike had already told us.

"I am sorry that Luke didn't confess before Mike had to shoot him," I said. "I guess now we'll never know with a hundred percent certainty that Luke was the one who killed Brick."

Gage smiled. "We know."

I raised a brow. "You do?"

"Remember the bullet that went through Brick's body, which the killer dug out of the wall?"

I nodded. "Yeah, I remember. Did you find it?"

Gage nodded. "It was in the glove box of Luke's truck. Not only did the guy keep the dang thing, he didn't even take the time to wipe Brick's blood off it. The lab matched the blood to Brick. It looks like we do have our hundred percent proof."

I couldn't help but grin. I loved it when everything came together in the end. Tony and I said our goodbyes to Gage and headed out into the sunshine. We were halfway across the parking lot when I saw a man standing just beyond the tree line. I turned to Tony. "Hang on. I'll be right back."

I walked as calmly and steadily as I ever had. I paused when I reached the spot where the man was waiting for me. "Dad?"

"Hey, Tessie. How is Mike doing?"

"He's going to be okay." I wasn't sure if I should punch him or hug him, so I just stood there doing nothing. "What are you doing here?"

"I heard about Mike. I was in the area and wanted to check on him. I couldn't go inside, but I figured you'd be along at some point. I saw your mother earlier. She didn't see me. She was with Ruthie. She looked good."

"Mom is doing fine. We all are."

A look of sadness washed over Dad's face. "That's good. That's what I hoped for. Listen, I can't stay long. I know you've been tracking me. I need you to stop."

"Why?"

"There are men who are piggybacking on your search. Men who are threatened by what I know and want me dead. They will stop at nothing and will kill anyone who gets in their way. For your sake, for Mike's sake, and your mom's sake, you need to let me be dead."

I nodded. "Okay." I glanced at Tony, who was watching us. "I need to go." I turned and took a step away.

"Tessie."

I turned back.

"I love you. I always have and I always will."

I could feel my heart pounding in my chest. There was so much I wanted to say, but instead, I just stood there and watched the man who had once given me piggyback rides fade into the forest.

Next from Kathi Daley Books

Preview:

Sunday, November 11

The moon reflected off the calm sea as I stood alone on the deck of the small cruise ship I'd boarded several hours earlier, with my best friends, Mackenzie Reynolds and Trevor Johnson. The trip had been something of a whim after Mac's new boyfriend, millionaire Tyson Matthews, had been given four tickets on the intimate ship, which held just twenty passengers. Ty had invited Mac, me, and Trevor, to come along for the voyage. It had taken a bit of finagling for the three of us to arrange to be away for an entire week, but it seemed too good an opportunity to pass up, so we did what we needed to do to make it happen.

Mac had just started her own software company and so had flexibility with her schedule, and Trevor had arranged for his manager at Pirates Pizza, the Italian eatery he owned, to cover for the week. What it had really come down to was my ability to find someone to look after my cat, Shadow, and dogs, Sunny and Tucker. Thankfully, my mother, Sarah Parker, who was already planning to visit my oceanfront home in the seaside community of Cutter's Cove, Oregon, for the holidays, agreed to arrive a week early. We'd lived together in Cutter's

Cove more than a decade before while in witness protection, so she had friends in the area, and as an artist by trade, she could never seem to get enough of the gorgeous sunrises and sunsets that could be found from her studio on the bluff.

"Lovely evening," said the ship's captain as he walked up behind me.

I turned and smiled at the tall man, whose gray eyes sparkled with merriment as he took off his hat, revealing short dark hair peppered with gray around the temples. "It really is just about perfect weather this evening." I held out a hand in greeting. "I'm Amanda Parker."

"Captain Armand Desmond." The man returned my offer of a handshake. "You are new to the cruise this year."

I nodded as a lock of blond hair blew across my face. "I am here with Tyson Matthews, who is a guest of Harris Hamilton."

"Ah," the man nodded, replacing his hat on his head. "I should have realized. Mr. Hamilton is a frequent passenger and I should have anticipated that he was going to be with us on this voyage. It is, after all, almost Thanksgiving."

"Mr. Hamilton always takes this same cruise?"

"Yes, so far he has. This is a good time of year for it. The ports are a lot less crowded than they are during the summer months."

"I guess not having to deal with the summer crowds is a plus. Is the weather always this nice?"

"Not always. Last year it rained during the entire week of this cruise through the islands, but we are expecting exceptional weather now. I hope that you have a wonderful time."

"Thank you. I'm sure I will. The ship is amazing, and I am looking forward to getting to know everyone."

The captain looked up at the sky. From his serene smile, I imagined he was relaxed and content with his life on the sea. He took a deep breath of the salty air, then looked back in my direction. "We are approaching Port Townsend, where we will dock for the next twenty-four hours. My co-captain has the wheel, but I should get back to help with the docking. It was nice to meet you."

"Thanks. It was nice meeting you as well." I waved as the man walked away.

After he left, I returned my attention to the sea. I thought Trevor, Mac, and Ty were going to meet me up here and wondered what had kept them. Not that I wasn't enjoying a moment of solitude. I liked the quiet and often sought it out, but tonight, under the stars, it seemed just a bit too perfect not to share. Sensing a movement behind me, I turned and watched as Trevor stepped onto the top deck from the stairwell and walked toward me. He'd dressed in black slacks and a dark gray jacket this evening, and with his dark eyes, long lashes, and thick dark hair, I thought he looked as if he could easily get a job as a *GQ* model.

"Wow. It is gorgeous up here." Trevor stepped up to the railing, took a position next to me, and kissed my cheek.

"It really is." I smiled in return. It was chilly, but not so cold as to be uncomfortable if you were bundled up.

"Have you been waiting long?"

"Not long." I let out a long, relaxing breath and leaned into Trevor's shoulder. "Have you seen Mac and Ty? I thought they might meet us out here."

"From their total absorption in each other during dinner, I think they had other things on their mind."

"Oh sure." I blushed, although I had no idea why. I supposed it was because things with Trevor and I were somewhat undefined, and any topic of conversation having to do with sex made me feel awkward and unsure, especially because we'd decided to share a cabin so Mac could bunk with Ty. "I did notice they seemed more interested in each other than in their lobster."

"It's understandable. It is a beautiful night and we are cruising on a luxurious ship where every possible want or need has been seen to. The stars are twinkling in the sky, the breeze is both warm and gentle, and the soft music playing in the background on every deck and in every hallway seems to have been selected to set the scene for romance."

"It really is just about as perfect an evening as we could hope for," I agreed. "At first, I wasn't sure the trip would be worth the effort of making last-minute arrangements, but I've always wanted to tour the San Juan Islands."

"Have you visited them before?"

"Once," I responded. "While I was in witness protection."

Trevor's smiled turned into a frown, and the tone of his voice changed from playful seduction to barely veiled annoyance. "Ah. I remember the two weeks of hell when you simply disappeared without a trace."

I placed my hand on Trevor's arm. "I'm sorry. You know I had to go."

Trevor let out a slow breath and then kissed my forehead. "I know." I could tell he was struggling to regain his previous mood. "And the past is in the past, so let's not dwell on things that no longer have the power to hurt us." Trevor's gaze narrowed. "Unless they do." He turned and looked me in the eye. "Any more texts?"

I shook my head. "Not a one." I forced a smile, although the familiar knotting in my stomach that accompanied any memory of the text I'd received a couple of weeks before could not be denied. The text had been sent from an unknown source and included a photo of Mario and Clay Bonatello, the brothers who had forced me into witness protection when I was a teenager. It also included a message: *She who spills the blood must pay the price.* Before they'd been murdered by their own family, Mario and Clay had worked for them. After I witnessed them killing a man in cold blood, they had set out to eliminate the only witness to their crime. I had been placed in witness protection and had thought myself safe until they found out where I was living and sent someone to kill me. Their discovery of my hiding place had forced me to run once again, which is when I had spent two weeks on Madrona Island, at the very northern edge of the chain. Eventually, my mother and I got a message from my handler, a man I knew only as Donovan, that the boss of the Bonatello family had decided he was tired of cleaning up the brothers' messes, so they'd been eliminated, and suddenly, after two years in hiding, Mom and I were free to return to our home in New York. I hadn't been back to Cutter's Cove until this past spring, when I returned to help solve the murder of a friend.

According to Donovan, he had no idea who had sent the text or why, but he had promised to keep an ear to the ground and let me know if he heard anything. I'd decided to go about my life and not to worry about things I could not control.

When I noticed Trevor's serious expression, I changed the subject to something a bit less intense. "When Ty said this ship was geared toward those looking for a luxury experience, I had no idea just how amazing it would be. It seems that no expense has been spared to ensure a first-class experience."

"It is pretty nice." Trevor's smile seemed to have returned as he leaned his forearms on the railing, then bent over just a bit to look down into the dark sea. The ship was traveling at a good pace, creating a fairly large wake that glittered in the moonlight. "I wonder how much the tickets for this cruise would cost if we'd had to pay for them. Given the intimate setting and the attention to detail, you know they couldn't have come cheaply."

"I'm sure the tickets were a pretty penny," I agreed. "The food, which has been excellent so far, would demand a hefty price tag if served in a five-star restaurant."

Trevor wove his fingers through mine as we stood shoulder to shoulder. "Tonight's meal was exceptional, and the staterooms are not at all what I expected from a cruise ship. I guess I was imagining something small and cramped, so I was pleasantly surprised to find that our room not only has its own Jacuzzi but the deck overlooking the water is pretty roomy."

I agreed the stateroom was pretty great. Personally, I was happiest about the fact that the sofa folded out into a bed. I wasn't sure I would have been ready to deal with the mechanics of sharing a room with Trevor if it hadn't worked out that we each had our own sleeping space. "It was really nice of Ty to invite us, but I have the feeling the other passengers all know one another. At dinner, it sort of felt like you and I and Mac were the odd ones out. I chatted with the captain briefly while I was waiting for you and he mentioned that Harris took this same cruise every year, but I wonder if the group as a whole has traveled together before."

Trevor leaned into me slightly. "I spoke with Ty earlier, while you and Mac were unpacking. It seems that the cruise is an annual retreat for Hamilton Investments, so yes, I would assume that the passengers, other than the four of us, all know one another."

While I knew that Harris Hamilton had given Ty the tickets, I hadn't been aware the cruise was a business affair. "So all the other passengers work for Hamilton Investments?"

"As far as I know, they either work for the company or have come as guests of a Hamilton Investments' employee."

"I wonder why Ty was invited on the cruise if it is to serve as a retreat for the company. Inviting outsiders seems like an odd thing to do."

Trevor put an arm around my shoulder. "Ty told me that he'd recently completed some computer updates for Hamilton and had stopped by his office to make sure everything was preforming properly. While he was in there, Hamilton's assistant came in to inform him that she had four extra tickets for the cruise this week because two of his employees were fired earlier that same day. Hamilton offered the tickets to Ty on the spot, and he accepted."

"Wow. I'm sorry to hear about the fired employees. I'm going to feel bad for using their tickets."

"They wouldn't have been able to use the tickets whether Ty accepted them or not," Trevor pointed out. "If he hadn't accepted them, they may even have gone to waste."

"I guess that might be true. But what a drag to think you are going on a cruise and then end up being fired just a week before you are to depart. I'm sure their plus-ones were bummed as well."

Trevor shrugged. "I'm sure it was a difficult situation, but we don't know the details, so I think we should put it out of our minds. The two people who were fired might have been stealing from the company or sharing classified information or participating in some other activity that warranted their firing."

I smiled at Trevor. "You're right. I heard there is dancing in the lounge. I don't suppose you want to try out some of your new skills?"

Trevor took his arm from around my shoulders and held out his elbow. "I'd love to take you dancing, but remember, my most consistent move seems to be foot stomping." He looked down at my feet, which were sheathed in strappy sandals. "I'd hate to mess up your pretty pedicure."

I laughed. "I think I'll survive." I'd been giving Trevor dance lessons since Halloween and he was progressing very nicely.

Recipes:

Orange Muffins

Beefiladas

Irish Stew

Brandied Cherry Cheesecake

Orange Muffins

Ingredients:

1½ cups vegetable oil
3 eggs
1¼ cups milk
2¼ cups sugar
¼ cup orange juice
3 tsp. orange extract
3 cups flour
1½ tsp. salt
1½ tsp. baking powder

Preheat oven to 350°. In a large mixing bowl, beat oil, eggs, milk, sugar, orange juice, and orange extract until smooth. Add in flour, salt, and baking powder and mix.

Line cupcake pan with cupcake liners (makes 24).

Bake at 350 degrees for 25 minutes, or until toothpick comes out clean.

Cream Frosting:

8 oz. cream cheese, softened
2½ cups powdered sugar
1 tsp. orange extract
½ cup heavy whipping cream

Mix cream cheese, powdered sugar, orange extract, and heavy whipping cream in small bowl. Beat until smooth.

Frost the tops of each cooled muffin.

Beefiladas

Ingredients:

2 lbs. boneless rib roast
Seasoned salt, pepper, garlic powder
40 oz. salsa (approx.) (I use half hot and half mild)
8 oz. diced green chilies
1 cup sour cream
8 flour tortillas
2–3 cups grated cheddar cheese

Trim all fat off boneless rib roast. Season with salt, pepper, and garlic powder. Place in slow cooker. Cover meat with store-bought salsa, either hot or mild, depending on preference.

Cook on high until meat begins to pull apart. Continue to shred meat as it cooks. When it's completely done (cooking time depends on size of meat and heat of slow cooker, but about 8 hours), spoon meat from sauce with slotted spoon. Reserve sauce.

Mix meat in a large bowl with diced green chilies and sour cream.

Place ⅛ of meat mixture in a taco-size flour tortilla. Place in a large greased baking pan (9 x 13).

Cover meat with reserved sauce *or* cover meat with canned enchilada sauce; in my family, there's a division as to which is preferable, so experiment a bit.

Cover with grated cheddar cheese. Bake at 350° for 45 minutes.

Irish Stew

Ingredients:

1 tbs. olive oil
1 lb. beef stew meat
2 cloves garlic, minced
1 onion, chopped
4 large carrots, peeled and chopped
¼ tsp. dried thyme
½ tsp. dried parsley
2 cups beef broth
2 tbs. butter, melted
2 tbs. all-purpose flour
1 tsp. salt
1 tsp. pepper

Mashed potatoes:

4 baking potatoes, peeled and chopped into large
chunks
6 tbs. butter
4 cloves garlic, smashed
3 tbs. milk

Brown the meat in olive oil. Add garlic, onion,
carrots, and spices. Cook for 5 minutes before adding
beef broth. Cover and simmer over medium-low heat
for at least 2 hours.

After about 1½ hours, make mashed potatoes.

Boil potatoes for about 20 minutes or until fork tender. Drain potatoes and mash with the butter, garlic, and milk.

Mix the melted butter and flour together. Add slowly to the stew.

Continue to cook for 10 more minutes.

Serve the stew over the mashed potatoes.

Brandied Cherry Cheesecake

Crust:

1¾ cups graham cracker crumbs
⅓ cup butter or margarine, melted

Filling:

4 pkgs. (8 oz. each) cream cheese, softened
1½ cups granulated sugar
⅓ cup whipping cream
1 tbs. vanilla
3 eggs

Sauce:

¼ cup butter or margarine
½ cup packed brown sugar
½ cup brandy
1 can cherry pie filling
1 tbs. cornstarch

Heat oven to 350°. In small bowl, mix crust ingredients. Press firmly in bottom of greased 2-qt. baking pan. Bake 10 minutes. Cool completely. Reduce oven temperature to 325°.

While crust is cooling, in large bowl, beat all filling ingredients except eggs with electric mixer on medium speed about 1 minute or until smooth. On low speed, beat in eggs until well blended. Pour over crust; smooth top.

Bake 90 minutes or until set.

Refrigerate until chilled.

In saucepan, melt butter. Mix in brown sugar and brandy. Heat to boiling over medium heat, stirring constantly. Stir in pie filling and heat to boiling. Add cornstarch. Boil 3 to 4 minutes, stirring constantly, until slightly thickened. Let cool slightly and then pour over cheesecake.

Refrigerate.

Books by Kathi Daley
Come for the murder, stay for the romance.

Zoe Donovan Cozy Mystery:
Halloween Hijinks
The Trouble With Turkeys
Christmas Crazy
Cupid's Curse
Big Bunny Bump-off
Beach Blanket Barbie
Maui Madness
Derby Divas
Haunted Hamlet
Turkeys, Tuxes, and Tabbies
Christmas Cozy
Alaskan Alliance
Matrimony Meltdown
Soul Surrender
Heavenly Honeymoon
Hopscotch Homicide
Ghostly Graveyard
Santa Sleuth
Shamrock Shenanigans
Kitten Kaboodle
Costume Catastrophe
Candy Cane Caper
Holiday Hangover
Easter Escapade
Camp Carter
Trick or Treason

Reindeer Roundup
Hippity Hoppity Homicide
Firework Fiasco
Henderson House
Holiday Hostage
Lunacy Lake – *Coming in 2019*

Zimmerman Academy The New Normal
Zimmerman Academy New Beginnings
Ashton Falls Cozy Cookbook

Tj Jensen Paradise Lake Mysteries by Henery Press:

Pumpkins in Paradise
Snowmen in Paradise
Bikinis in Paradise
Christmas in Paradise
Puppies in Paradise
Halloween in Paradise
Treasure in Paradise
Fireworks in Paradise
Beaches in Paradise
Thanksgiving in Paradise – *Coming in 2019*

Whales and Tails Cozy Mystery:

Romeow and Juliet
The Mad Catter
Grimm's Furry Tail
Much Ado About Felines
Legend of Tabby Hollow
Cat of Christmas Past
A Tale of Two Tabbies
The Great Catsby

Count Catula
The Cat of Christmas Present
A Winter's Tail
The Taming of the Tabby
Frankencat
The Cat of Christmas Future
Farewell to Felines
A Whisker in Time
The Catsgiving Feast
A Whale of a Tail – *Coming in 2019*

Writers' Retreat Southern Seashore Mystery:

First Case
Second Look
Third Strike
Fourth Victim
Fifth Night
Sixth Cabin
Seventh Chapter
Eighth Witness

Rescue Alaska Paranormal Mystery:

Finding Justice
Finding Answers
Finding Courage
Finding Christmas
Finding Shelter – *Coming in 2019*

A Tess and Tilly Mystery:
The Christmas Letter
The Valentine Mystery
The Mother's Day Mishap
The Halloween House
The Thanksgiving Trip
The Saint Paddy's Promise

The Inn at Holiday Bay:
Boxes in the Basement
Letters in the Library
Message in the Mantel – *April 2019*

Family Ties:
The Hathaway Sisters
Harper
Harlow – *May 2019*

Haunting by the Sea:
Homecoming by the Sea
Secrets by the Sea
Missing by the Sea
Betrayal by the Sea – *March 2019*

Sand and Sea Hawaiian Mystery:
Murder at Dolphin Bay
Murder at Sunrise Beach
Murder at the Witching Hour
Murder at Christmas
Murder at Turtle Cove
Murder at Water's Edge
Murder at Midnight

Seacliff High Mystery:
The Secret
The Curse
The Relic
The Conspiracy
The Grudge
The Shadow
The Haunting

Road to Christmas Romance:
Road to Christmas Past

USA Today best-selling author Kathi Daley lives in beautiful Lake Tahoe with her husband Ken. When she isn't writing, she likes spending time hiking the miles of desolate trails surrounding her home. She has authored more than seventy-five books in eight series, including Zoe Donovan Cozy Mysteries, Whales and Tails Island Mysteries, Sand and Sea Hawaiian Mysteries, Tj Jensen Paradise Lake Series, Writers' Retreat Southern Seashore Mysteries, Rescue Alaska Paranormal Mysteries, and Seacliff High Teen Mysteries. Find out more about her books at www.kathidaley.com

Stay up-to-date:

Newsletter, *The Daley Weekly*
http://eepurl.com/NRPDf
Webpage – www.kathidaley.com
Facebook at Kathi Daley Books –
www.facebook.com/kathidaleybooks
Kathi Daley Books Group Page –
https://www.facebook.com/groups/569578823146850/
E-mail – kathidaley@kathidaley.com
Twitter at Kathi Daley@kathidaley –
https://twitter.com/kathidaley
Amazon Author Page –
https://www.amazon.com/author/kathidaley
BookBub –
https://www.bookbub.com/authors/kathi-daley

CPSIA information can be obtained
at www.ICGtesting.com
Printed in the USA
LVHW041221190519
618379LV00036B/1631/P

9 781798 641316